MW00711566

Bloodletting
&
Fruits of Lebanon

Also by J. Eric Miller:

Animal Rights & Pornography
Short Story collection

Bloodletting

and

Fruits of Lebanon

Novellas

by

J. Eric Miller

Edited by Beverly A. Jackson

Cover art work created by Candace Carman

Lit Pot Press, Inc.
3909 Reche Rd. #96
Fallbrook, CA 92028

Printed in Canada by Stride Print Services

Library of Congress Cataloging-in-Publication Data

Miller, J. Eric
    Bloodletting & Fruits of Lebanon
Fiction - novellas
Library of Congress Control Number 2005900962

ISBN #978-0-9743919-9-1

4

Acknowledgments

The author wishes to thank:

Dane, whose birth and life have been lessons in love.

Jodi, who saw these works through, too.

Rita El Habr, who gave time and energy to a stranger simply because he asked.

Margo Lakin-Lepage via the Kennesaw State University Press for looking at the manuscript when I couldn't see it anymore.

And Beverly Jackson, the editor every writer deserves but few meet.

Bloodletting

"What about Lanada Cutfinger?" I ask John Elkheart. He's been telling me about what has happened during the five years I've been gone. "Where did she go?"

"You still got a thing for Lanada?"

I lean against the bar. All around us people I used to know talk and drink. A few shoot pool. Every now and then, one or another of them drifts up and says hello, but nobody seems surprised to see me and not many ask me where I've been or what I've been doing.

"Just curious," I say.

"I think it's been a couple of years since I seen her around her. Her family still got the place up Dry Creek." He takes a drink of his Bud Light. "Did I mention Twilite Wyse had her car wreck some time back?"

"I heard that," I say, and I have, but I don't remember from whom, and I can't picture her, not exactly. She'd gone away, to can pineapples, I think, and she'd come back, like everybody does, and started working at Natural Resources, stuffing pollen into capsules, shipping them around the world.

John takes off his dirty red and white Marlboro baseball cap and adjusts the bill. Then he puts it back on.

"Where was it she went?"

"Hawaii."

"Why Hawaii?"

"Somebody came through, recruiting. Airfare, a place to stay, hard work. That must be the farthest away from here just about anybody, even you, got, ain't it? They had a bunch of Indians and Mexicans down there. Hawaiians treated them pretty nice."

We drink and John tells me about Dallas Morgan who drove into the woods in the middle of last winter and then got out of his truck and sat beneath a tree and froze to death. He tells me about Shelia Graybird, who went to school in Charlo, and how she took her three kids into the woods and laid them down with pillows and blankets and then ran a hose from the exhaust pipe in through the window and then got inside and died with them. Her suicide note was addressed to the father of two of the children. They printed it in the paper. In it, she'd written that she felt he was destroying himself and her only recourse was to join him.

"It said at the end, 'I'll race to heaven.' People couldn't figure out why she took the kids, but I know," John says.

"You know?"

"She probably couldn't stand to think of them trying to make it without her. When you kill yourself it's after you decide the world is a no good place. Who wants to leave someone you love in a no good place? It was like a mercy killing. Anyway, she was a good ball player. Beat the hell out of our girls. You remember her?"

"I think so," I say. But in truth I don't remember her, not her talent, her face, or her name. I'm still trying to picture Twilite Wyse, trying to picture Dallas Morgan, trying to picture the others John has.

Mike Saint-Juste takes the barstool beside me and says, "Hey."

"Hi, Mike."

He orders a Bud Light.

"I was telling him about what's happened around here," John says.

Mike nods. "What were you, down in California?"

"LA," I say. "Los Angeles."

"Yeah, that's what they said," Mike says, blinking heavily. This blinking is something new about him, or at least I think it's new. "You come back now, did you?"

"He's looking for Lanada," John says.

"No," I say. "I'm just passing through."

Mike lifts his beer from the bar. John says, "He don't like the old story where you go away and come back again. He's got this new one to tell about India, ain't it? That's his story. Think it's true?"

Mike's eyes squeeze closed and then slowly open. He drinks from his beer and says, "What's that? India?"

Chad Montoya's father comes up and hits me on the shoulder and asks me if I remember the match I wrestled with Timmy Dumontier from Mission my senior year. I nod; a little unsettled, because I hardly remember the match at all. As far as I recall, it wasn't that great a match. I wasn't a great wrestler. I wonder how he remembers it, or even me, and why. He hits my shoulder, says it's nice to see me, and moves up the bar.

John nods after Chad Montoya's father and says quietly, "And you know about Chad's wreck. You know what they say, if they'd keep cars off the rez then Indians would live forever."

Mike finishes his beer and orders another one. When he gets it, he blinks heavily and says, "Good to see you," and walks away with the fresh bottle.

I turn and order a shot of vodka for myself and one for John. We drink them without clicking them together, as I would have done with the people I know in Los Angeles. John gets us each a beer. I glance up and at the mirror which is dimly lit and warped and I don't like the color of my face it.

We both turn around and watch the people in the bar for awhile. Most of them went to school with us, though there are fathers and mothers and brothers and sisters of our classmates as well. Some of the younger patrons have faces I think I recognize by family resemblance or just as grown up versions of kids I used to see running around. There are a few full bloods, but almost nobody on this reservation is pure Indian. First the French trappers came from the north and east, spreading seed and some of them settling, and then the missionaries came and began to convert the Indians. After the reservation was established, whites bought up a lot of the farming land and they bought land to build houses close to the lake. Though there are all colors of skin, hair, and eyes in this bar and on this reservation, I realize, looking around, everybody's Indian, everybody's the same.

Then I think, "Wait."

I think, "Not quite everybody." Though my mother is full blood, I feel like one who doesn't fit. I must have once.

I glance back at the mirror. Why am I so pale? Haven't I been dark all my life and where has the darkness gone? I take a long drink from my beer and study the faces of these people to see if anybody studies me. Occasionally I catch a quizzical glance or a smile but nothing that feels like it means to say I am a stranger.

Or, for that matter, that I belong.

"Well, what the hell else?" John Elkheart asks absently.

Lisa Fiddler has come up to stand beside him and is looking at me. The last time I saw her, she was fifteen or sixteen, thin and pretty. Now her cheeks are heavy and her body has rounded into the shape of a teardrop. She's smiling at me and I'm glad the smile is exactly the same as I remember it, and I'm glad that I remember it at all.

"They said you come around. Come up from California. What you doing down there? Going to school?"

"Yep."

"Finish?"

"They gave me a degree."

"A degree, huh? "

"Yeah." She doesn't ask me what kind it is. That's all right. I don't want to tell her. I don't really want to tell anyone about it. I don't want to try to explain the vagueness of a BA in Communication or the classes I took to get it. It hardly mattered there and it doesn't matter at all here.

"Los Angeles, huh?"

"You bet," I say. Her familiarity eases me. I try to think of something to say that will be of interest to her about where I've been, but nothing comes to mind.

"Well, so, you're back." Lisa says, leaning toward me. Her breath smells of a sweet liquor. I try to remember if I ever had a thing for her or if I ever thought she had one for me. It wasn't so long ago, five years. These things should not be hard to remember. I'm tired from the trip. I'll feel differently when I have slept. I'll wake and know if the decisions I think I've made are the right ones.

"Just drove into town today," I say.

Her eyes are the color of candy root beer barrels, the kind my father used to buy around Christmas. I try to muster some feeling for her, something like lust, though I don't know exactly what that would accomplish.

Lisa asks, "What are you, going to stay with your dad awhile?"

"A few days only."

"I've been catching him up," John says, "before he heads off to India. That's what he says, anyways. Think he'll really go?"

"Hey now," Lisa says, "Chuckie just come in. Did John tell you we got married?" She holds up her finger, but I don't look at the ring.

"Nice seeing you again. Maybe if you're in town long enough, we can have you over to the house."

"Okay," I say.

As Lisa walks away, John says, "They're in the development. You seen it?"

"Looks like the only part of town that's grown."

"That's not growing," John says. "That ain't development, either. Hell no." His face goes blank and he drinks from his beer. After a moment, he says, "She's still a cute one, though, ain't it?"

"Yeah."

"Should have asked her about Lanada," John says. "She'd know."

I watch Lisa and Chuckie, who has also gotten fat. They stand facing each other for a little while. Her mouth is moving and his is still. She throws up her hands and then folds her arms. Chuckie shrugs and looks up and sees me and nods and I nod back.

"Allan White is in Deer Lodge for killing some folks in Missoula on a drunk driving. And so is Larry Freeny for chasing around this white girl up in Kalispell he says was his girlfriend. Let's see, and Charlie Jack for raping a couple of thirteen-year old girls is also in the prison. Shit, he did that while you were still here only it didn't come out for awhile. You know what they say about Deer Lodge, the other rez."

I know it could go on like this, the ritual of stories told about those who have stayed to those who have returned: the list of dead and jailed; the list of married and divorced; the mothers; the supposed fathers; the names of others who have left and those who have come back. I haven't been to this place I ought to call home for four years, and the only visit before that I cut short, to just a few days. There are no real changes. Although the names may be different, all the stories have already been told before and will be told again. I've heard them. If I hadn't left, I'd be telling them, and, eventually, they'd be told about me.

"Little Thomas will be looking for you."

"Not at the bar."

"Yes he will. He'll come right here if it means finding you."

I know John is right. He drinks. I drink. Across the room, Mike blinks heavily. Chuckie and Lisa stare at each other.

"You hear from Lung much, you being so tight and all?"

Lung is Jason Lungren. Jason and John and I hung out together in high school. At some time or another during the last four years, my father told me that Jason married a girl from Frenchtown and started up a log home building business. In fact, my father has probably told me all of the things John Elkheart told me just now. I quit listening to my father at some point. I guess it was when I couldn't put the right faces—or, really, any faces at all—on the people in the stories. I must have intended to really leave this place and I must have done a pretty good job of it.

"We fell out of touch."

"Yeah, well, me too," John says. There is bitterness in his voice. In fact, there has been bitterness to him even while he is laughing since the moment he came in.

"Why's that?"

"I say the hell with Lung." John drinks. It has been only a few years, but there are lines on his face that it looks like it should have taken twenty to grow. I'm tempted to seek out my own face in the mirror again but I resist the urge.

"What happened?"

John pulls the cap down so the bill blocks out his eyes. He says, "What I can't figure out is why he didn't ask me to go into that building business with him? I know it's a tough row, but hell, he's got a chance with it. I wouldn't mind a chance. I was the one who put him on the idea of it to begin with. You know he's in Helena right now."

"I would have liked to have seen him."

"Is that what you come back here for?"

I shake my head and am pretty sure that this is true. But I can't say what I've come back for, who it is I think I need to see or what. In any case, there is a short list of the people I should try to visit. John is one, and that is now taken care of. There's Little Thomas, who I don't want to see but am certain I must, and Rob Skyburns, to whom I owe an apology and from whom I wish to get the location of a grave. There is, of course, Lanada Cutfinger, but I can't really imagine seeing her. That leaves Jason, and he's out of town.

"Anyways, I think that covers it," John says, "the five years you went away."

He shrugs and looks around the bar as if he has suddenly been infected by my fatigue. Behind me is the drive from Los Angeles and then this night of drinking in the blur of faces of people I have known in a life that is almost my own, this last long hour of short explanations about my recent return and quickly approaching departure.

Little Thomas has come through the door. Some problem in his bones stopped him from growing above five feet. He had the name Little Thomas when my family moved to the reservation, and there was a Big Thomas, though he died dirt biking before we graduated high school. I don't know if they started calling Little Thomas "Little" first or Big Thomas "Big". Maybe it happened at the same time. In any case, people greet him and move out of his way as he heads toward me.

"Speak of the devil," John says under his breath. When Little Thomas is closer, John turns to him. "How's it hanging, Little T?"

Little Thomas doesn't look at John. He reaches for my hand and grips it. We shake. Though we were not close in high school, he began to send me letters about a year after I left for California. Those letters didn't stop until I hadn't answered him for two years. He didn't seem to want an answer, anyway. He would write me with the same kind of news John Elkheart has been sharing with me now, the same kind that my father was sharing with me then. He wrote to me that he thought I'd gone on a journey to find an answer that I might bring back and with it to save the people on the reservation from whatever it is he thinks they need to be saved. I am worried that he has come to collect that answer.

"You wanna beer?"

Little Thomas keeps one eye on my face and the other peels away and glares at John Elkheart. I've never seen anything quite like it. I look down at my nearly gone beer and try to calculate how much I've had to drink tonight and if I should stop.

"Aye, jokes. Still a sober man, ain't it?" John Elkheart grins sheepishly at Little Thomas, whose eye returns to me and looks warm again.

"How's your mom?" I ask.

"She's real good."

Little Thomas's mother is a high school teacher who gives Indian Studies and classes in the Salish language. She is a full blood and very pretty. After she showed us *Soldier Blue* in class I fantasized for weeks that it was the olden days, I was a Cavalryman who had rescued her from the bad soldiers, and we made love. Other times, it was still the olden days, but I was an Indian brave and rescued her from the bad soldiers and we made love. Perhaps those were my first sexual fantasies, but I cannot remember with certainty if that is true or not. I

14

think again of Lanada and this makes me drink, even though Little Thomas makes me feel self-conscious about drinking.

"So are you going to do something with your Native American Studies?"

"I took that because I thought it'd be easy. It's only a minor."

"You can do something with that."

I think about the classes I took to fulfill the requirement. I learned about some of the intricacies of tribal politics and the relationship between various tribes and the federal government, and I learned about issues of sovereignty, land, and water. I studied statistics on suicide, alcoholism, and poverty in classes that tried to ferret out reasons and come to solutions from sociological standpoints. I studied the history of various tribes and the history of the Indians as a whole and even the history of my own tribe, the Flatheads. I read theories about how the Indians were undone not by mere force but by disease; by the slaughter of buffalo; by their unique perspective on the goals of war; by their naïveté; by their pride and jealousies; by their inability to unite. I look around the bar at the people in the near dark and I think none of what I learned would mean much to anybody here.

"I was sorry to hear about your divorce."

"Divorce?" John Elkheart hollers. "Some storyteller you are. Left out a little bit, ain't it? You been married and divorced already? You might be a rez kid after all, ain't it?"

Little Thomas says, "I was sorry about that. Your dad said also there was a baby . . . ."

"A baby?" John is so loud now everybody close is staring and those on the other side of the bar glance over. "We been drinking here for just near three hours and I tell him every goddamn detail about the rez. And he don't tell me he been married, divorced, and that he's fathered a kid." John whistles.

I say nothing, hoping it will pass. I think about my wife and boy, one and a half years old now. Martina and Jake. She was Danish and in Los Angeles working as a nanny. We met when I was twenty and lonely. I liked the sound of her voice,

15

the way the first time she called me, she spelled out the two
and the threes of her phone number so that I would not
confuse them. She got pregnant quickly. We married quickly.
My father came. Her parents came. They didn't like me. It
wasn't long before Martina and I found out we didn't like each
other much, either. Or maybe she just didn't like me. I can't
remember. Or I can, but don't want to. She and Jake went to
Denmark to live with her parents. That was a year ago, and we
haven't spoken since then, though she sometimes sends my
father pictures of Jake.

Little Thomas says, "Anyway, I could guess it must
have been hard on you. It was hard on him, your dad, her
taking the baby back to Europe. I go over there and sit on the
front porch with him sometimes. He gives me ginger ale."

John squares up to look at me. His face is serious. I
notice again the lines on it, especially those coming from the
corners of his mouth. He says, "I bet you're mad, ain't it?"

"No," I say. "I'm not mad."

"Shit, I'm mad and I ain't been divorced."

"It wasn't a good match."

"I ain't even been married. No baby. Nobody taking
anything like that from me."

He's peering at me as if he wants something, but I
don't know what it is. He whistles again. Then he says,
"Everybody's mad. Don't you get mad?"

"I don't know what to be mad about," I say.

"Everything," John says. "It all. "Everybody's mad,
loading up guns, loading up cars . . . ." A darker shade seems
to come over his face and he peers around but doesn't seem
to see anything that eases him. He pulls the ball cap off his
head and wipes his face with it.

Little Thomas steps closer to me. "I want to talk to
you about something. What your dad told me, that you're
going to India." His eyes shine and I wish that John would say
something to cause one of those eyes to peel away again and
thus cut Little Thomas' concentration on me by half, but John
just stares into his hat and Little Thomas continues to stare at
me. "Why do you want to do that?"

16

"I'm going there to teach people to speak better English. They're opening all kinds of technology jobs up to them, but they need better English to do it better."

Little Thomas gives a disapproving jerk of his head.

John has looked up and seems to be glaring at me. I wonder what the anger is that I see in John's eyes. I realize that despite the fact we've been drinking together, talking, and even laughing, there has been some underlying tension between us. Maybe John sees how out of place I am. Maybe he sees that I'm trying to think of how I used to talk so I can do it again and not sound as if I don't belong. Maybe he sees that I am embarrassed of my button-down shirt and my tan slacks. Maybe he sees that I ought not be here. Maybe he thinks I never should have been here to begin with. Maybe he wants to call me out—not for going away, talking, dressing, and even thinking differently, but for coming back.

Little Thomas says, "Just because that woman left you don't mean you have to run that far away."

"That's not it, Thomas," I say. "I'm not running."

From the corner of my eye I can see a ragged red blob. For perhaps a year now it has been appearing once or twice a week. It started out the size of a pinhead but it is about the size of two fists now. Maybe it is some problem in my eyes, or maybe it is some problem in my imagination.

Little Thomas says, "You shouldn't cross the ocean. You'll disappear if you do that."

"Disappear?"

"You'll be gone."

John put his hat back on his head. The anger is not all together gone from his face but it is no longer focused on me. He says, "Hey Thomas, ain't you heard of the internet and computers and all? He can be in goddamn Russia and you can hear just as much about him. Ain't you heard of even letters and the postal service? And airplanes and ships? What do you think? Think it is smoke signal days and you got to be on the next hill over, ain't it?" John smiles around though nobody but Little Thomas and I seem to be listening. "Haven't you heard of growth and development?"

I put my beer bottle on the bar behind me. "Thomas," I say quietly, "I'm going there because it feels like the thing to do."

I realize, even as I say it, that part of me doesn't believe that. I want to believe it. At the same time, since making the arrangement, I have had bouts of a serious doubt. I can feel it now. It is hard, almost impossible, to believe that I'll really make the plane. The idea of me in India seems fantastical; the idea, in fact, that there is an India at all seems absurd. Part of me believes I am looking for an excuse not to go. Or that I'm trying to fall into some kind of trap which will keep me here.

On the rez.

Where I am not comfortable.

Where I do not belong.

I can hear John Elkheart ordering each of us another beer. It's my turn to pay. I pull out my wallet, take the money out, and give it to the bartender. After a few swigs, the red blob is gone.

"You came back for a reason. Just like that last time."

"I came back then because it was Christmas," I say. "And that was the only reason. And that was four years ago."

"You left again for a reason too. You left early."

"How do you know?"

"Your father. He knew you could have stayed longer. I know what happened. You took off so fast that time and didn't come back because you were afraid. You wanted to stay here and that scared you. You know where you belong."

"You think I belong here?"

"You had to go get something. Now it is time for you to bring it back. Come and do something good with your education before all these people are lost."

"What are you talking about?" John says. "You wanna make him out to be something he's not?"

"You don't know what he is," Little Thomas says.

"You want to make him something nobody is?"

"Little Thomas," I say, "you can't lay that on me."

18

"I'm not laying it on you. It's just there. You laid it on yourself."

"I didn't bring anything back. I don't have anything for anybody here. I'm not going to save anybody. Hell, if anything . . . ."

"If anything what?" John asks.

"If anything nothing."

Little Thomas looks away from me.

The bar crowd has thinned out. Chad Montoya's dad slaps me on the shoulder again as he passes. It is a hard slap that I can feel through my shirt as if it were on my bare skin.

"Clear out," somebody yells. "Get out."

John Elkheart and Little Thomas and I amble onto the porch, where we can smell smoke. Many places in the West are on fire this summer. The Bitterroot Valley to the south has been razed, and a forest to the west of the reservation has begun to burn.

Chuckie and Lisa are against the far post. He's got his back to it and she's crumpled in his arms with her head collapsed onto his chest. I imagine she is asleep though I can hear the sound of her speaking softly. Josh Winter Hunter is pissing off the other end of the porch and a small group of people are standing around talking.

"Should do some smoke jumping," Casey Groulet says. "That's where the money is. These firefighters, some of them go and start some of these fires. Then they get to go to work. Make enough in one summer to live good all year. Natoni Peaks, didn't he go off for smokejumper training? What happened to him?"

"Got killed. Burned up, that's what," somebody says.

"No," Mike Saint-Juste says, blinking. "It was the smoke that killed him. Inhalation."

"Shit, man. We'll see it soon enough, right here. Wind River down in Wyoming is on fire. I got a cousin there."

"You got cousins everywhere."

"We all do, ain't it?"

"Everything is going to burn."

The porch light goes off.

"Hey," John says, "I got a case at my house. Who's coming?"

I see the nodding of heads in the dark. I say, "I'm too tired. I got to get to my dad's and get in a good night's sleep."

People wander off the porch and start toward their vehicles. "There's the tribal money," John says, indicating Cameros, Firebirds, muscle cars, and pickup trucks. "What they give you if you make eighteen. Everybody gets a fucking car, ain't it?"

"You really mean it?" Little Thomas asks me quietly.

"I've got nothing," I say.

His eyes fall. His face appears to fall. In fact, I think he may very well fall. But he doesn't. He turns away. John kills off his Bud Light and sets it on the windowsill. It is, I think, the last time I will see either of them. This gives quickly away to the suspicion I felt earlier in the night that I will not really leave for India but will rather stay here and, in fact, see John and Little Thomas and all the others most every day the rest of my life. I look away from the two of them. In the darkness the shapes of the mountains are defined by the end of the stars. The creek gurgles and there is the sound of insects. A warm wind picks up.

"Thomas," I say, "where's Lanada Cutfinger?"

"Lanada? She was running around with René DeFrance, last I heard." His voice is soft and sad.

John slaps his forehead. "René DeFrance," he says. "That's right, ain't it? They went up north, I heard."

"René DeFrance?" I say. "I always thought he was the kind to leave."

"There is no such person," John says. "Except you, if you're right about you."

We walk off the porch.

"I got to go," Little Thomas says.

"I'm sorry, Thomas," I say.

We watch him walk toward his car. John says, "Up in Polson. Lanada and René DeFrance."

I close my eyes. René DeFrance. I can see his face, clearly, which is not the way I see the faces of the other people

John Elkheart has been talking about. It is not even the way I see John Elkheart's face itself. I can see no face, not even my own, with the clarity with which I now see René's. I see his light skin, his green eyes, his reddish hair. René's family moved to Ronan just a little while after we moved here, but I remember suddenly that I knew him long enough to know I didn't like him. It was the way he looked, the paleness of his flesh and eyes, the redness of his lips.

Perhaps it is my fatigue, or the beer, or my simple and hard to explain and just now intensified hatred for him, but I have the strange and certain sense—or maybe it is a wish—that René DeFrance and I are headed toward a showdown.

The drive from the White Buffalo Bar to my father's dirt driveway can be no more than a mile and a half, but it seems to take a long time. After I park in front of the house, I walk back to shut the gate and see that Rose Lockhart is sitting on her back stoop. She's lived in the trailer close to the other end of this driveway since my family came to live here and probably for a long time before that. I can envision it no other way. She is an old and stooped woman with a small unhappy mouth set in a mess of wrinkles that are like webs in a window around a bullet whole. She has never been friendly with me or my father, nor was she friendly with my mother when my mother still lived here. I remember sometimes hearing laughter from inside her trailer at night. I never knew who she laughed with or what they laughed over. It was frightening then and the specter of her in this darkness is frightening now.

There's some sound, hard to place, but when I'm still for a moment I realize that she is muttering as she sits there. Her glasses catch the moonlight, making her eyes smears of yellow, which seem to search to separate me from the darkness. Her muttering grows louder and I worry this means she has seen me, and I worry further that her mumbling is directed at me in the form of a curse. The town behind her is dark, and even the street lamp is so dim that it only seems another kind of darkness.

I step out of the drive and into the shadows of the pine tree along the fence. I believe her head turns to follow me. The mutters grow louder but the words are no more distinct than when she was quiet. Maybe she speaks the old language. Whatever she is saying, I can hear her anger. She is angry at me, and I wonder why. I think she's always been angry at me, and at my family. I think she's always been weaving chants of loss against us.

"Hey," I say quietly, much more quietly than even the quietest of her murmurs, "what do you have against us?" I've meant to say "old lady" at the end of this question, but it does not come out. I don't mean to know about her anger, anyway. I am afraid to know. I am, in fact, afraid to know anything about her. I keep to the shadows as I sprint toward the house. Going through the front door, I can hear her voice, the only sound in town, the only sound in the world. It is loud enough now that if I were by the fence again I could know what she is saying.

Inside, the house buzzes, as if her noises have been picked up and translated into something else. I piss. Fear is still in my guts and I consider vomiting but I know it isn't going to get out that easily. The door to my father's room is open to pitch blackness within. I go slowly through the living room, trying to compose my thoughts and regain my courage. I tell myself that I've been here before, many times, and that I know the carpet beneath my feet and this configuration of furniture. I tell myself that I have walked up the stairs from the living room to my own room enough time as to make those steps so familiar that I cannot have lost them nor will ever be able to. There is the faint and familiar odor of my father's pipe and that puts me at ease.

Upstairs, my room is hot. I sit for a long time on the bed. I remember hearing my first summer Pow-Wow, when I was ten. I remember the beating of the drums in the burning night. They scared me. I knew better than the cliché of Indians from TV westerns, and, of course, I knew my own mother was an Indian, and therefore, I was an Indian to some degree or another as well. Still, the persistence and steadiness of the sound made me afraid. I lay awake in the hot, pounding dark. When I finally achieved sleep I was still aware in it of the drums. There were several nights like that.

I lie back now. Everything is quiet. Though I am fatigued, I can't imagine sleeping. Last night, I slept in a hotel in Utah. Or I think I slept. I can't quite remember. The night before that, I was in Los Angeles. The city disintegrates as I think about it. Buildings shimmer and disappear slowly. Palm trees melt. The ocean leaps from its shell and hovers. There were people with whom I worked and went to school, and they threw a small party for me. That was several nights and one thousand years ago. Now these people I will say were my friends are dim in my mind, shadowlike.

The ground trembles.

The ghosts suck up into the sky.

The waves crash.

LA is gone.

I had to leave it. I knew that even before I found a way out. I had finished school. For the last four years, I'd worked part time in guest relations at CBS studios. After I graduated, the job became a full time position with a full time salary and full time benefits. I was poised to move further up into the system. There were younger versions of me down the ladder and older versions of me up the ladder. I could see clearly where I was going and where I had been. I realized that LA was supposed to be my home, though I didn't feel at home there. I was missing something. It wasn't just Martina and Jake, or the idea of what I was supposed to have with them. It wasn't the reservation or the people I knew here. It wasn't my father or my mother. It was the unknown thing I've been missing since before I left them or this place to begin with. I suppose I believed I'd find it in Los Angeles. Whatever it is, that thing that is missing, sometimes I tell myself I had it once, that I can have it again. Maybe through some return, or some grander departure.

I sat by the big window in my apartment in LA, considering it all, trying to decide what to do about that longing, and the phone rang.

The woman on the other end told me she'd been given my name by one of my professors. She asked if I would be interested in teaching English in India. The ground literally shook. I thought it was an earthquake. Maybe it was. I believed the skin of the world was preparing to roll back and reveal something new beneath its surface.

So LA is behind me.

"Here I am," I say out loud. And I am here, lying on this bed I used to know, in this room I used to know. In this place that is supposed to be of transition only. I think of the people I saw tonight. I think of the people I didn't. There is Lanada Cutfinger, up in Polson, with a man I want to style as my enemy. There is Jason Lungren, building log homes in Helena.

I want to miss him. I want to regret that I won't see him during this visit and thus probably ever again. I want to feel nostalgic about the times we shared. I want to think of the stories that connect us. They don't really feel like they belong to even a part of me, but, at this moment, I want them to.

I tell myself the beginning of a story. It is about the time Jason and I bought a real firework from one of the dealers who came through the reservation and sold 4th of July stuff in little booths and put together big displays for the towns. What we bought was one of the display class fireworks, a rare and magic thing to have, and we didn't know what we'd do with it. That winter, we met two girls at a wrestling dual off the reservation in a town called Hot Springs, and we made a date with them. Our plan was to set the firework off as surprise, the strength of which would cause them to surrender to us completely. The girls were supposed to meet us at a restaurant in Charlo but never showed, and so we went by John Elkheart's place and picked him up and went driving.

I close my eyes and put my hands over them, trying to concentrate on the story. I can remember it better than I would have guessed I can. I can remember it so well that I can see it; I can almost feel it.

We started into the mountains, on old logging roads covered in snow and ice. We drank beer and did not talk much about why the girls might have chosen not to meet us. Finally, we found a field with the snow evened out looking pure and pretty underneath the stars. John was so drunk by then he climbed in the back of Jason's truck and lay down. Jason and I tramped into the field and pushed the cardboard base of the canister into the snow. We lit a long fuse and ran back to sit on the hood of the truck.

"What the hell you doing?" John called

"Something which was supposed to get us laid," Jason said. "Get up and look."

Then it burst. It wasn't as large as we expected, but it was brighter than I'd imagined. It was a flower of blue in the sky, then the shards of it sizzling as they came down, and then there was blackness again and the stars, and the night was very quiet.

"Fuck," John said.

"Those girls didn't deserve that," Jason said.

"That's fucking magic, what we did."

"We should do this every year, just the three of us," Jason said. "Come out here to this place exactly and light one just like that."

We drank beer and watched the place in the sky where the firework had exploded. The snow was smooth and blue. Even our tracks couldn't be seen in it. I believed we would do what Jason suggested. I believed we would get together every year for the rest of our lives and shoot a single blue bloom into the night. I believed those things even though I was getting ready to apply for colleges, even though I was preparing to move on.

I feel cool now, as if the snow from that night and that night itself are truly with me. I feel that sense of nostalgia I've been looking for. It is a good feeling, and somewhat frightening. I have learned to fear things I miss, or might miss. There are all these necessary losses and I do my best to avoid

25

the pain associated with them. And yet, at this moment, I am glad to know that I miss the idea of me and Jason and John out there in the snow putting on our yearly one-round firework show.

I tell myself that tomorrow I will swing by Jason's house and introduce myself to his wife. I will see the two kids I've heard he has. I'm not sure it will mean anything. Maybe even seeing him wouldn't mean anything. I can't think of what seeing John Elkheart meant earlier tonight, or what seeing any of the others meant either. Tomorrow, I will see Rob Skyburns, and I will offer him an apology and ask him a question. There is something beyond forgiveness or the location of a grave that I want from that visit, though that something else is not yet clear to me. In truth, the bulk of the reasons that brought me back here are unclear. I think I came to say goodbye, but to whom, I'm not sure. To all of them, I guess, all the people I've known and imagine I will not know again, my father amongst them. Perhaps I have come to say goodbye to some version of me as well. There is the me that might have stayed—that might have returned.

And if I'm really honest, I realize that the me who might have come back, or who might not have ever left, is not fully dead. I see that he tries to convince me to find away to belong again, or to belong at all. It is he who has told me the story so well. I know what he is doing with it. He's trying to make me stay. He's telling me to find what was lost, where it was lost, and never lose it again.

I am too tired to think like this. I am only confusing myself. There is nothing for me here. I have made a choice to go into a future, to cross oceans and find a new world, some place that must be better for me and offer me more than the places I've been.

The night after tomorrow, I will be on a plane. I have to.

I make a globe spin in my head. I focus on India. Then I say the word, "Bombay."

If I sleep, I will dream of India, but now I am afraid that I will not sleep.

Then I do sleep, but not well enough to dream.

26

There's the sunlight in the morning. I feel the sleepiness of this town. I see my suitcase on the wooden floor. The bees from the hives at Natural Resources are rising off the grass. I stand at the window with my eyes slit against the light slanting in. Somewhere below me, my father still sleeps. And waiting for me in this day is Rob Skyburns, his dead brother Fred, perhaps the last ghosts I need to confront before I move forward.

The Skyburns home is a doublewide trailer with wooden siding. The green paint is more faded and peeled than the last time I saw it, but it's the same place it's always been. I reach through the frame where rusted tatters of what was once screen hang and knock on the wooden door behind it. There is no sound from within, and I get off the cinder block step and walk a little ways onto the lawn that is more dirt than grass and try to peer up through the windows. Rob opens the door. For a moment I can't clearly see him, as if he is backed by the sun or as if there is a mist between us, though neither of these things is true. My eyes are tired. I put my fingers against the lids and hold them there for a second. When I open my eyes, I see Rob clearly.

"Hello," I say.

He looks more the way I remember him looking than anybody I've seen since coming back. He has shoulder-length black hair. His face has not aged, though it was always marked by frown lines and almost always expressed a sort of perplexity, which made him seem older. He is half Blackfoot and darker than most of the Indians here. Though Rob is not a traditionalist—doesn't dress in the olden ways for Powwows, doesn't beat drums or dance or speak the old language—he has always struck me as more Indian than any person I know.

"Come in."

Inside, we walk past his mother, who lies on the couch. Her face and hair are the same color of gray. She looks dead. "Hello, Mrs. Skyburns," I say quietly.

"Hello, Sean," she says, opening her eyes.

"How are you, Mrs. Skyburns?"

"Rob is taking care of me. Rob?"

"Right here, Ma."

She smiles at him.

"You want a ginger ale, Ma?"

"No. You and Sean go and have a good time."

In the kitchen, I ask, "Who's Sean?"

"I don't know. Maybe it's from television or her dreams or her memories or something."

In silence, Rob fries a piece of baloney for each of us and puts those pieces between slices of bread.

"You want cheese?"

"No, thanks."

Rob takes a large can of mixed nuts from the cupboard and pours some into a bowl. He takes the bowl to his mother. Everything—the bread, the nuts, the baloney—is commodity, bulk food the government distributes every month to any tribal household that wants them. When I was young, I understood that the difference between commodity food, which comes in black and white packages, and the regular food my parents kept at our house, was a mark. It was one amongst many. There was the difference between the trailer homes like Rob's, or the development homes on west side of town, and my family's home: a large, white, red-roofed ranch style house built by the first white merchants in the area. Though I was able to see the differences, I had trouble putting a finger on what meaning they were supposed to have. As I think about it now, feelings of resentment and appreciation toward those differences that duel in me.

We take our sandwiches back to Rob's bedroom, which looks exactly as it used to, except that a framed picture of Fred hangs on the wall. The twelve-inch black and white television is still on a stand close to the end of his bed. His

28

Atari machine is still attached to it. In the machine is a Pac-Man cartridge and I ask Rob if it still works.

He grins for the first time since I've arrived. "Yeah, but you can't see the Pac-Man at all. I don't know if it's the TV or the machine or the game itself, but he's invisible."

"Pac-Man is invisible?"

"I move the joystick around watching the dots disappear. You get a feel for it. It's like *he's* the real ghost. Like he formed the magic of disappearance."

He sits down at his desk on which several notebooks are stacked.

I sit on his bed.

His grin fades and he asks me what I've been doing. I tell him. Los Angeles, school, India. I keep going. I tell him more than I've told anybody. I tell him I don't eat meat, and I apologize for letting him make me a sandwich. I tell him that I've come here for reasons I'm uncertain of. I tell him that I was married briefly and divorced and that I have a child I don't imagine I will ever see again.

"Have you got pictures?"

The question surprises me. "No," I say. "My father has."

"What's his name?"

Again, I'm surprised at the question, perhaps because nobody else has asked it. "Jake," I say.

Rob nods. I feel as if I've said too much or not enough. I ask, "What about you?"

"I went up to the community college for a couple of semesters. That was after I got out of the Marines."

"I heard you'd joined."

"I did that right after Fred died. And Dad was still alive and I wanted out of here. But it wasn't how I thought it was going to be. I missed this place. I acted crazy and they let me out. Maybe I was crazy."

Rob and I hung out together very little, and his brother Fred and I, even less. I spent time with them mostly the summer my family moved here, before I'd met Jason and John and the others. The Skyburns were sort of outcasts, Rob by choice and Fred because he took special education classes in which he was the only student. I would visit them as a kind of break after I made other friends. At those times, Rob and I would simply talk. Fred would sit by, smiling, usually, as if he was following the conversation and it amused him, though he did not really follow it. We'd eat fried baloney and drink Kool-Aid. I've tried for the last three or four years to remember some of the content of the conversations I had with Rob, but I can't. I remember the tones of his voice. I remember that he almost always seemed serious. I remember that sometimes he would go on with a type of rhythm which caught and held me, a rhythm that I felt long afterwards, remaining in the sway of maybe not the words and their meanings, but of the sounds alone. Perhaps as much as it is that I want to apologize to Rob and that I want him to tell me where to find Fred's grave, it is for those sounds I want to see Rob. What I intend from the visit to Fred's grave, I do not know. I think of all the other dead and the fact that I am not drawn to their graves. Then I think that I am in fact drawn to their graves, that in Fred's grave perhaps I mean to see them all.

"When I came back from the Marines, my dad said to me that everybody runs. He was pretty much dying then. He said that Whites run toward what they don't know and that Indians run toward what they know."

"Whites toward what they don't know?"

"And Indians toward what they do. He said it didn't matter. He said all places we run to in this world are bad." Rob looks at me. I believe that he is trying to see if I am white or Indian, as if to know to what I am running. Then I realize I'm only projecting that search onto him. After a moment, he looks away from me and at the picture of Fred. It is a high school photo. There is a stand of aspen trees on a large mat behind Fred. He is wearing a light blue shirt with shiny buttons. His glasses are large and round, and he is grinning broadly. I remember that shirt. I remember when we lined up to take those photos. It's soothing that these memories are so real and feel so much to truly belong to me.

"I'm sorry I didn't call you or send a card or something," I say. "I meant to. I even thought about coming back for the funeral. I really don't know why I didn't do any of those things. I'm sorry. I know it sounds too simple when I say it, but I really mean it, that I'm sorry."

"It's okay."

I feel slightly unburdened, but I know I have not gotten everything from this visit I need. Rob does not stop looking at the picture of Fred. He says, "I was working at Natural Resources. Fred did things to help Ma around the house. He was changing pipe and throwing bales, too. You know. One day he went for a run. He had this idea that if he put on some tennis shoes and his red shorts and went out running he was really doing something. That made him happy."

"I remember. It did make him happy. He's probably the only person I know that always knew how to get happy."

"Yes. He'd come back so tired. He come back sometimes after being gone for an hour or more. I'd think maybe he forgot, you know, to stop. Or to turn around. He would just kind of get lost in the run. But what happened, what made him die, wasn't because he went too far or too long. There was just something bad in his heart. He was born with this defect. I might have it too. They asked me to be tested, but I said no. I got home from work and he wasn't here and Ma got home and she was worried. Pretty soon Stan Steiner's little brother came riding on his bike real fast down out of the hill and across the river. He come riding right up to the front door and tips over his bike and says, 'Fred is lying out there on the road and won't move or anything.' And that's just how Fred was, too, lying there like he fell asleep, really peaceful. There were these pine needles in his hair."

"He was good," I say.

"He was innocent."

"I want to see his grave."

"It's not in Mission with the others. Ma wanted him buried out at the old cemetery. Dad's out there too."

"I'll go this afternoon. Do you want to come?"

"No."

"All right."

I think about standing up and shaking hands and saying goodbye. I don't know what else to say to him or hear from him beyond what I've said and heard. The idea that in a few days I am supposed to be in Bombay and that I may never see this place again, comes over me. At this moment, it seems more absurd than it has at any other time. I fold one leg over the other. I wait for whatever else it is that I need from my visit with Rob to come to me. It does not come, so I say, "You went up to the community college?"

"Yeah, I took a couple of classes in Native American history and modern politics. Reservation issues and all, you know. I also took creative writing courses. I liked those." His eyes open a little wider and he smiles more than grins. Then he puts his fingertips to his lips as if he is slightly embarrassed.

"Why did you like them?"

"I'm writing stories now. They make me happy. First I get an idea, and then I think about it for a long time. Days, maybe weeks. Whatever I'm doing, I think of the story. I'm thinking of one now."

"What kind of story are you thinking of?"

"The story I'm thinking about in my head is about a band of Indians who cross the ocean during World War I. Did you know that the Iroquois Nation really declared war on Germany when the United States did?"

I do know that, but I shake my head as if I don't.

"That's right. They had a council and discussed it and then drafted a declaration of war that they sent to Germany. In the story I'm thinking of, a war chief and half a dozen braves build a Viking style ship. Did you know Vikings were the first Europeans to have contact with Indians?"

Again, I shake my head as if I don't know.

"Yeah, they got on okay and exchanged a few ideas, but, you know, they were both warlike people and one thing leads to another. I mean, I suppose they never felt at ease with each other and often they would get to fighting. You can just imagine it. The Indians in their old time gear standing there

32

facing down a bunch of Vikings all dressed up I guess the way they are in the movies, with their axes and spears and shields. Those most have been some battles."

As he speaks, his frown lines become less evident and his face does not look as perplexed as it normally does.

"Anyway, this band of Iroquois design a ship, a kind of cross between the Viking ships they've learned about and the traditional canoes they've built for years. They use this ship to cross the ocean. I know what to do with them on the water. The trip would be a spiritual quest and each of the braves would accomplish something during it to bring him into full preparation for the war in Europe. Each would face internal and external obstacles and overcome them, and as a whole they would overcome the challenges of the journey. But I don't know what to do with them when they get to Europe. Perhaps I should have them storm a beach and get chopped down by rifles. Or maybe they should get exposed to a European disease which would wipe them out immediately."

"Those are grim endings."

"Yes. I know. I know it would be nice if they could give a disease to the Europeans instead, or if their bow and arrow approach could overwhelm the enemy, but it never worked that way. Maybe they would meet some French soldiers—the French were always the best with the Indians, you know—and form with them a heroic battalion. I don't think it worked that way much, either. It's nice to not know the ending yet. It gives me something to think about."

"I like that story, Rob. I would read it if it were written."

He smiles. It is a shy smile. He looks more like Fred in this moment than I've ever seen him look. I glance up at the picture.

"Do you have anything finished I can read?"

He looks at me blankly. Then he smiles again. He gives me a notebook and opens it to a page toward the middle. Maybe I've never seen Rob's handwriting before. Maybe I just never paid attention to it. The flow of the letters is beautiful. Staring at the page is like looking at a drawing or even a dance.

I sneak a peek at Rob, but he has gotten up and turned his back to me. I begin to read.

The story is about a modern Indian who dreams a time machine into existence. He ponders over how to use it and finally has a vision in which he should travel back through history and meet the original white settlers. He takes an AK-47 and explosives to this meeting, and he kills all the whites and sinks their ships. He comes back to the future expecting things to be different. But nothing is. Again, he sits pondering and finally has a vision in which he should go back in time to the signing of the. treaty which signaled the end of his tribe's freedom. He goes, as the vision seemed to suggest he should. There, he kills everybody, Indians and whites alike.

When he returns, he is surprised to find himself still on a reservation. He is the same as he was before and so too are the people around him. He tries time and time again to change the world in which he lives by going into the past, but nothing works. No matter who he kills or what he destroys, he always returns to the present and finds it just the same as it was before. Finally, in despair, he sets the time machine for the date of his parents' wedding. He comes into the reception carrying a rifle. His father is young and half-drunk. His mother is young and six months pregnant. He recognizes uncles, aunts, cousins, and grandparents. There is a large, round, white cake, only one tier high, but very bright. Crepe paper hangs around.

Nobody pays him any attention. He begins to shoot them. He shoots every present carrier of blood, semen, and egg that could produce anything like him. He expects his mind to go blank, but it does not. Though they are full of holes and covered in blood, the people continue to move around and act as if nothing has happened. Frustrated, he watches them leave the wedding. He watches for nights and days as their lives continue, the wounds always visible, though nobody ever pays them any attention. He watches so long that he watches his own life begin. And he watches his own life until it catches up to the present from which he begins his journeys into the past. There he kind of bleeds into his life again and is himself again.

34

He wakes. He tells himself that he did some good. He tells himself that he died almost the instant he shot his mother, and now he is having an extended death dream. The fetus lives in the dying mother for perhaps three seconds, but in those three seconds, it dreams the story of them all, and it dreams a life for itself. The person in the story then realizes that he is living this dream and that soon, perhaps, the dream will end. Perhaps he will be walking by the side of the road. Suddenly, cars will disintegrate before him. Faces will come apart. Everything will fade, and he will find himself sucked back into that dying fetus and he will then see blackness and that will be all. Knowing this makes him feel better. That is where the story ends.

I look up.

Rob has turned from the window and is watching me. "Did you like it?"

"It's sad, Rob."

"Yes."

"Are you sure it makes you feel good to write like that?"

He doesn't answer me. After a moment, he says, "If you could take just one thing back that you've done, what would it be?"

I know what it would be. My father gave me a ring when I left for California. It had come with our family from Norway, through Iceland, New York City, other places. It belonged to people I've never heard about. It was so old that all the carvings on it were worn down, and you could just see the faint outlines of them. It was always loose, and one afternoon I went with some friends to the beach to throw a football. It must have come off then. I don't tell Rob all of this. I say, "I used to wear this ring. I'd put it in a safe place. Some place it couldn't be lost from."

He nods solemnly. He says, "The things we lose. I don't know what I would take back. I tell myself sometimes that if I could put myself with Fred that day he died, I could change it. But I don't really believe I could change it."

There is no color to his face. No real color to his hair. I blink. I want to bop the side of my head to clear the color back in. I glance around his room and everything looks gray. I think about the outside of the house and to me everything looks gray there as well. I am overwhelmed with the gray. I look down on the blue writing on the page and am relieved to find it still beautiful. I think about the words and the story and the sadness there, and everything grays all over again. I look at Rob and know his life will not change. The house will decay. His mother will die. But every day will be the same for him. I think about the others I have seen again on this trip. They are wound up in the gray too.

This is a stagnant place. I try to imagine that things were good here once. I try to believe that I felt good here. I try to know what it is that I really came for. I think of LA, which is not cast in gray, but black. I think of India, which has no color at all, which at this moment is just a smear of white light in my mind's eye.

I say, "Rob, what did we used to talk about?"

He takes the notebook from my hand and folds it closed and puts it on the stack of the others.

"What did we used to talk about?" I ask again. I don't like the anxiousness I can hear in my voice.

"What do you mean?"

"We used to talk. When I'd come see you, we'd talk for a long time. Don't you remember? We'd talk and talk. What was it about?"

"I don't know," he says. "We were kids."

The road is empty. I pass fields of alfalfa where lines of pipe lie and spigots from the pipe pump burst water into the sun. I look back, to the west; the mountains are spotted with open patches left from logging operations. Those clear cuts are connected by the thin lines of roads carved into the forest. It makes a pattern at which somebody could stare and from which that somebody could be tempted to try to find meaning. A thin layer of smoke lies over these mountains and it occurs to me that they will burn. The clear cuts and the roads that connect them and the forests from which they were made will be razed and made equal.

I look forward, to the east. The mountains there are not cut up, nor are they covered in smoke. They are dark with pine and tamarack. I can see the white church at the base of those mountains. It is toward this church that I drive. Old Chiefs are buried there, alongside veterans from all the wars, and tribal people whose names are still around, and tribal people whose names have faded out.

And there is Fred.

I find his grave. It is a white slab of stone, remarkably thin, with his full name and the date of his birth and the date of his death. There is no sense of him here. I feel no ghost, not of him or any other. I crouch and wait for something, but I still feel nothing, as if the people buried here did not live and did not die, as if Fred, whose life I want to be certain of, did not die, and did not live. In missing him, I feel his brother, Rob, pull away from me too, as if he is already buried here, in a grave that also gives no real feel of his life or death, as if Rob, too, has not lived and will not die.

I look all around, at the tombstones and tin crosses and the simple steel plaques, past the graves of babies with tiny picket fences gone brown, above the wrought iron fence and the white church and the fields beyond. I look to the western mountains that have grown hazy with smoke, and then I look into the sky where a single white cloud hovers.

I feel heavy and entrenched.

I try to imagine I am headed some place, which I am, that I will leave this ground, which I will, but I feel that I may not really go and that there is nothing I can do to make this or any journey. Against this helplessness, I cannot cry out. And I cannot cry within.

I drive.

There is the old high school of cylinder brick painted yellow. On it hangs an athletic emblem, a wooden carving of a faded Viking helmet. Everything looks much the same. The paint flakes off the bleachers that stand over the football field to the north. The grass is dry to the point of hardly seeming grass at all. I circle around and pass the basketball court where the hoops are still rusted chain only half attached and the asphalt is split by weeds and small trees. The dirt parking lot is deeply rutted, a shallow pond during a hard rain. The elementary playground to the south is full of equipment that does not work and is posted with warnings.

It is not possible that at one time these things were not decayed—that at some point people stood here seeing these things new and believing in the newness of these things. The chain nets had to have been bought and hung in rust. The parking lot nor the courts could ever have been smooth. The swings, the slide, and the merry-go-round must have always been crooked and cracked and dangerous.

My father's house is only two more blocks to the south, but I take the long way around, crossing onto the main highway and passing the now closed down Joe's Station. Its windows are not boarded and signs advertising products still hang behind the cracked glass. It looks no more or less dusty or decayed than it ever looked. I find it hard to believe that inside it is now empty. Or perhaps it is the opposite that is hard to believe, that people ever worked and shopped here.

Further down, a group of teenagers is playing rap music on a boom box and trying to look hard in the parking lot of Joe's Restaurant, which is also shut down but which also looks like it was either never really open or closed. A few of the kids have long hair, one of them wears it in braids, but most have short hair slicked back. They all have unlaced sneakers, sports pants, and muscle shirts, and some of them even have muscles. When I lived here, you would find kids in the same places, but they would have been wearing flannel shirts and faded out satin Viking jackets and jeans. Past them are the remains of Stockman's Bar, which burned from the inside out when I still lived here. Next to that is a building painted brightly in several colors with a sign that reads Natural Furniture. A guy with a long blond beard and square glasses sits on a lodge pole bench

38

out front and glances up at me. I figure him for a credit card hippie from Missoula, and I know how it will go for him: he'll hang with the Indians for awhile, get bored or disillusioned, and go back to college. He's always sitting there, always has been, always will be; his face will change, and his hair and the shape of his spectacles will vary, and the name of his shop will be different from one year to the next, but in essence they are all one man, a man the Indians know and are even fond of.

I stop at the post office and can't find my father's box. Its location comes to me only as I mean to give up and walk out. Then it's a matter of the combination, which also comes to me only when I have the feeling that I will never remember it. Save for a letter I sent from LA, the box is empty. I recognize my writing, and the address from which I posted the letter. I wrote it three weeks ago, an announcement of my intentions to leave LA and this country for a new world, and a promise to come home and see my father before I go. It must have been sitting in this box for some time, and it worries me to realize that my father is not checking his mail. It worries me further to think that he is getting no mail save that which I send him, not even junk.

Now, I feel certain of nothing.

I have the urge to open the letter and read it as if it were written by someone that knew more about what he was going to do and why than I now know. As if maybe it tells a truth that I have somehow since writing it lost and which I can get back if I only read and believe it. I put the letter in my breast pocket.

Leaving the post office, I bump into Kean McCrea. He wasn't at the bar last night and so we greet each other for the first time in years. A plaster cast goes around his chest and over his shoulder and down his arm, which is held out at an angle by a brace, the other end of which is stuck into the cast on his chest. I tell him I'm in town for a couple of days and ask him what he's been up to.

Waving the left side of his body, as if he means to indicate his arm, he says, "See this? Got it busted up."

"How'd you do it?"

"Me and Jamie Englishman figured out since all the old cottonwoods in town are dying we could make some money topping them. We never done a thing like that before but we figured it pretty good. One guy on a ladder with a chainsaw, the other guy on the ground with a rope. The way we did it, Jamie would cut most of the way through the top of the tree and I'd pull the rope that was tied above the cut. That way I can direct it, get to fall where we want it. I pull and get the hell out of the way. We was going to get all the trees in town. Your dad's, they're all bad, they all need to be topped. But we were at the old Demur place and Jamie was up on the ladder and he was cutting through the tree. He'd tied the rope above the cut. I was standing there with the other end waiting. But what happened, the tree snapped back and kicked Jamie in the face. He yelled out and I panicked and just pulled the rope hard. I wasn't ready though and so I froze after that and then when I tried to run I got all tangled up and the tree fell on me."

Kean points with his right hand to his left arm and shakes his head and laughs.

"I thought I was going to die. I said to myself, 'You are about to meet your Maker, ain't it?' Shit if I can remember a thing from then on. Jamie, his jaw broke, he drove us both up to Mission to the Indian hospital and they done a real fine job. See?"

He taps the cast again.

The story itself has been visible, the tree kicking back into Jamie's face and then falling on Kean. But now as I try, I can see nothing before that described moment, nothing of Kean or Jamie from the years we spent in school together, often in the same classes. He is before me now, and I can see him, but I know that when he is not before me I won't be able to see him, except for in the story he just told, as if that is all there is of him.

"It's good seeing you, though," he says.

"Should I help you with your box lock?"

"No. Hell, I drove here. I can open the box."

"It's good to see you, too. Hope your arm gets better."

He smiles. It is a sincere smile and it strikes me that he is happy here, that he is fulfilled, that, in fact, it is not all gray here, that there are people like Kean who have made of it something good. Why should it seem like a bad idea for me to stay and to learn to stick?

Kean turns, and as he does, another story blooms. I cannot remember who told it to me, if it was John, if it was my father, if I heard it some other way. It is about Kean's younger brother, who shot his girlfriend and then himself about a year ago. I cannot tell what is the true story of this place, the one that Kean's smile seems to tell, or the one that is told by the splatter of blood on the wall in my mind.

I get back in the Jeep and drive back the way I came, past the place that is for now called Natural Furniture, where now another guy, much like the first one, sits alongside him on the lodge pole bench. There seem to be twice as many kids looking hard outside the Joe's Restaurant. Further down, Joe's Station is still shut down.

I'm close to the developments but I don't want to drive through them. I turn south and head past a few trailer homes and a half block of shacks. Then there is the Demur house, the site of Jamie and Kean's accident. Their treetop still lays in the yard. It is a tall white home much like my father's—in fact, my father's house was a Demur house, which is to say it belonged to one of the old Demur brothers before we bought it—with pine and cottonwood trees in the yard and white walls and a red roof, and an altogether Midwestern look. I suppose that Mr. and Mrs. Demur are dead, though it is possible that they are sitting inside right now.

I keep driving. Ketty Wilson stands by the side of the road, waving. She has a big smile on her face, the other half is nearly consumed by tortoiseshell glasses. At first I am startled because I believe her name has been on some list of dead given me by my father or John Elkheart or Little Thomas. I wonder if I am confusing her with one of the others, or if she is in fact dead and it is my projection of her spirit I see. And I wonder why, if I've caused a vision of her to stand by the side of the road waving and smiling, I've done that.

I stop.

Ketty walks over to my side of the car and puts her hands on her hips and shakes her head. Then she says my name.

"Ketty Wilson," I say. She's not dead and I am not projecting her. I feel a sense of relief grand enough to make me smile—almost grand enough to make me laugh.

"They said you'd come back."

"Not for good."

This makes her shake her head. I almost ask her why but don't. I ask, "What's new?"

"I married Tommy Maceck, from Ronan. Do you know him? Both of us got to working out at Natural Resources."

"What are you doing there?"

"Same thing they were always doing. Making little capsules of bee pollen. Shipping those pollen capsules all over. All the way to Japan sometimes. Me and Tommy both. You know how it is. Most all the working Indians work there. Course all the money goes to some white guy who owns the place." She puts her hand to her mouth. "No offense."

I wonder why I should be offended. The reference to it makes my smile and my impulse to laugh disappear.

"Tommy and me, we're right over there." She points to a small brown house with a well-kept yard full of small, white dogs. It used to belong to a French teacher we had for a couple of years when I was in high school. I can't remember her name, or her face, really, but just the general impression she gave of always being frazzled. Nobody signed up for French. She moved, unable to sell her house, which was still vacant, when I left myself.

"What else is new?"

She shrugs, still smiling. She always smiled, I remember. She is, in fact, more smile than anything else. It brings to mind Kean's smile and I think of the warmth that exudes from both of them. For the first time, it means something to me. "Nothing really," she says.

I glance down the road. When I look at Ketty's smile again, it frightens me. There is too much comfort in it. Although I know the smile is sincere, it feels like a trick—not one she is playing on me, but one I am playing on myself. In this trick, I tell myself that there is a possibility for real life here, that from the gray I can create—or maybe it is recognize—real color, a color which will never be consumed black or wiped out in light.

She shakes her head. I don't know why and I don't ask. Her smile doesn't falter. I'm drawn toward it but I want to get away from it. I can feel the weight of my foot on the brake. I can feel the muscles of my leg tighten to lift my foot away, and I have to will them to relax.

She says, "My father's staying with us for a while. Can't use his legs really, just like a couple of logs under him."

"I'm sorry to hear that."

"My dad has had himself some fine times. He was real happy as a young man and so now the sadness and the anger balances it. That the way of it. Why don't you come over and say hi to him and meet Tommy?"

I say, "I can't right now. I'm heading back to have dinner with my dad. It was good seeing you."

"He still over by the school?"

"He hasn't moved."

"I guess I see him around sometimes but it seem like he stays in pretty much."

"That's him."

"So you're not going to stay?"

"I'm basically passing through. But it was nice seeing you." My foot lifts slightly.

"Hey, you know the fires? One of them crossed over last night, up in the northwest part of the reservation. These fires, nobody can stop them. Maybe nobody wants to stop them. You know how it is. There's a lot of people like it that everything is on fire this year. They say it should be that way and that good things will grow out of the ash."

"Good things out of the ash?"

"That's what they say about fires."

"I hope all goes well with your father," I say. "It was nice seeing you."

"I hope all goes well with your father, too." Her smile broadens now. She waves me away. I will race home. I will hide myself there refusing to believe in the illusion of something here that I did not find before and can now find; I will remember that my future is in the unknown, that it is in the white light, and not this gray. I will.

Tammy runs after the Jeep. I stop for her again.

"You looking for Lanada Cutfinger?"

My face must be blank because my mind has gone that way. Finally, I say, "You mean driving around looking for her right now?"

"I mean that's what you are doing."

"Lanada Cutfinger?"

She smiles wider than ever. "Oh, I remember, I could see. She's up in Polson now, with René DeFrance, married. I don't know where, exactly, but maybe her dad could tell you if you give him a call. Though I don't think they get on too good. She hasn't been down this way in a long time. Couple of years, at least. Good luck."

She waves me off again and I go. She's told me nothing new about Lanada, but I feel as if I've just discovered something fresh and startling just the same.

There is a long line of trailers, and past them a dirt road, which winds into the hills to one side and meets with the highway on the other. Following it toward the highway, I pass a small home painted dull blue. It was abandoned for a long time, but I know Jason bought it several years ago and has fixed it up. In the yard is the woman who must be Elizabeth, his wife, short and blond-headed, big of belly as if with baby. She is picking up a gallon jar of dark brown liquid I know to be sun tea. A toddler wearing only a diaper is close to her, and there is another child of four or so sitting sullenly on a barstool close to the fence. That one, the oldest, must have been the one she was pregnant with when they got married. There is something negative in me, a sort of weight I can feel. It has grown out to counteract all Ketty's dangerously positive energy. That necessarily negative thing tells me that Jason and Elizabeth seem to be having a baby every year and a half or so. It tells me that they do this because they couldn't think of what else to do after the first, and so had another and thus a cycle began there. And that this cycle will go on like this forever, through them and their children. Clothes are hanging from the line and I see that he wears flannel shirts and she wears sundresses and that everything is faded—the yard, the walls, the kids, the woman herself. I drive a little more quickly, meaning to pass her and the children and all of it, but I can't keep from looking again.

The eyes of the oldest child rise to me, and I see his father clearly in the shape of his face, though the kid is lighter skinned than Jason is. And Jason is pretty light. Elizabeth looks up as well, and I feel like she has recognized me somehow. So as not to hurt her feelings and Jason's when he hears of it, I should stop and pretend as if I intended to introduce myself all along. Then her eyes sweep past me as if she has recognized nothing of significance in my presence.

I look back at her as I go. I look back at the kids. This is the house where Jason Lungren lives and these are now his people. They might have been mine.

I used to know him.

Once, we shot a firework off and it bloomed blue into a patch of the sky and that blue reflected down on the snow.

But I don't know him or his people or his place, anymore.

There is that ragged red circle, bigger than it has ever been, in the corner of my eye, and I am more clearly afraid of it than I have been before. I can almost feel its weight like a gravity that means to pull me, or gravity's opposite, some force that means to push me away, to tip me over. I can feel that it means to grow bigger and encompass me eventually. I can sense that it will spread through my eyes and mouth and I will be gone.

I drive fast now, trying to keep my mind off the red, trying to keep my eyes from sliding to the side as if to fully perceive it.

And then I think of Lanada's name, and am reminded that I can know how to find her and I can go see her there if I really mean for this trip to be whatever it is I mean for it to be.

I wonder sometimes if my father had set himself on marrying an Indian. He grew up in Indiana to full blooded, second-generation Scandinavians: my grandfather's family straight from Norway into New York and then to Michigan and then Indiana; my grandmother's family, also originally Norwegian, from Iceland, where they stayed two hundred years, then directly to Indianapolis. My father's father made a deal with him when he was eighteen. It was if he went to college for one year, his father would buy him a new truck. He could do what he wanted after that year. What he did was drop out of college and drive his pickup to the Yukon. There, he lived on an Indian Reserve for over a year—I don't know which one. I don't know what happened to him there, who he met, what he did, or why he returned to the States. I try to imagine his existence in the Yukon. Perhaps he fell in love with an Indian woman up there and somehow it didn't work out so that he looked for her again everywhere he went; perhaps then he saw her in my mother. Or perhaps his heart, for some reason, had always been bent on an Indian woman and that was one of the reasons he went to the Yukon Indian Reserve to begin with. Or perhaps he just fell in love with my mother by coincidence.

The truth behind it all doesn't matter. What I know with certainty is that he loved my mother, even after she left him.

In any case, after he left the Yukon, he married my mother; they had me. He moved us to a small mining town in Colorado where he worked his way into the position of shift boss at the mine and spent a lot of his off time in the mountains. He became a hunter, or maybe he'd been one already in the Yukon and took it up again in Colorado. My mother said that my father had itchy feet and that was why he tramped around the mountains. She said that frequently, and she always said it with a smile, so that I understood it as something about him that endeared him to her.

My mother is full blood Salish, but her family moved to Seattle during the time the government sent aggressive agents on missions to encourage Indians to move off the reservations and assimilate into white society. My mother's father was anxious to go to Seattle—I don't know why; I don't know if my mother knew why—and she grew up there. That's where my father, returning from the Yukon, met her. I know nothing of how specifically they met, their courtship, the proposal. Is this important knowledge? Does my lack of it mean anything? Martina often complained that she did not feel she knew me, though I tried to tell her stories that would reveal something of who I was. When that didn't work, I explained that I was raised according to an Indian tradition that maintains to know is more important than to be known. I tried to tell her I didn't even know myself.

My mother and father and I lived in that small mining town in Colorado for ten years. Underground with explosions and echoes of explosions and the pumping of pumps and the rattling of jack hammers, my father's ears suffered. He developed tinnitus. The mine offered him a settlement. Then he asked my mother if she wanted to go back to her people. She didn't know what he meant. This is the story she told me of how we came to live on the reservation. She told it not long before she left. She said, "He had his mind set on this place." By the time he'd asked her if she was ready to return to what he called her people, he'd already spoken with a real estate agent in Missoula. He already had his eyes on the house on the Flathead Reservation in which he still lives. We moved.

After a year, my mother drove into Missoula three times a week to attend courses at the university. My father seemed comfortable with this. He seemed comfortable with everything. He repainted the house. He worked on the fence and the lawn and slowly cleaned out the three outbuildings. He bought chickens and raised them and dug up a patch of yard for a garden in which he grew corn and green beans, squash,

47

potatoes, and cauliflower. He liked to walk through town and lean on fences and talk with people. He began hiking and hunting in the mountains as he had done in Colorado.

When my mother left, I was seventeen. My father was thirty-seven. I don't think either of us saw it coming or understood. She went with one of her professors, to Virginia. I've only met him twice, the second time during the wedding of my own ill-fated marriage, and his face from that ceremony comes clearly to my mind, much more clearly than my mother's does. Her face, too, will come, or I'll want it to, before this trip is over, but now is not the time for that. Her departure was as sudden and unexpected as a car accident, the way things are on the rez, where the people seem used to the rhythm of long uneventful periods followed by sudden unsuspected and unwanted shifts; where people seem used to these slow beats to quick tragedy. A person is alive, eats and drinks and does everything else every other person does, and then in the course of a minute one morning, that person is dead. A building stands for three decades and then in an evening burns to the ground. Your mother, your wife, she is there, and then she is gone.

When she left, my mother took almost nothing, as if her old things had no meaning for her. A year after she had departed, just as I was preparing to go to California, my father put those things my mother had left in boxes.

My father's forty-three now, but he looks older. The property is decaying as well. He used to build little dams along the stream and manage them so that it would flood and water the cottonwoods, but he hasn't done that in what I guess to be years and the tops of the cottonwoods have died and turned brown. Half the eastern fence is sagging. Knapweed has overtaken the yard. The outbuildings are in all manner of collapse. The garden is just a patch of grayish earth. His kitchen dishes are not really clean, the windows are spotted, and there is grease caked into the tile around the stove.

It's been four years since I've last seen this place and five since I lived here. Dust is everywhere; more dust than it seems could have accumulated in four years. The dust is so much that I wonder how there can be anything left of the things from which the dust is made. When he greeted me upon my arrival, with a handshake and a hug, I noticed that even the skin of my father's hands seems to be turning to dust.

The dinner table sits before a picture window facing east. A bird feeder half full of pink liquid hangs outside. That he has recently remembered to fill it gives me hope for my father. He serves slabs of meat I don't recognize, potatoes cut into eighths and fried, biscuits from a mix, and green beans poured from a can into a gravy boat. I dish up some of everything but the meat.

To the side of the table is a chest of drawers that has been in my father's family for two hundred years. It was shipped across the Atlantic and then dragged across the country, generation by generation, until it came to rest and wait here. I can see the side of my father's face reflected in it. Beside my father's face, my own is visible. Our faces have much the same shape; they are elongated with deep holes where the eyes are. What strikes me most is how white I look, whiter even than my father. All my life, I thought of myself as being dark. In Colorado, where we lived was predominantly Latino. There I believed I looked like the Latino kids. Here, I believed I looked like the Indian kids. In Los Angeles, I felt I looked like any number of minorities. I felt, in fact, like the perfect minority. It is as if some bad magic has overtaken me since I came back to the reservation and is causing me to pale. I am whiter now than I was in the bar last night.

"Are you all right?" my father asks. His voice has grown choked over the last few years, as if his throat is collapsing. He also speaks loudly. Each time he came to see me in LA—three trips in all—he told me that the roaring in his ears had gotten louder. "It sounds like I am walking toward a stream," he said during the last trip. He was smiling as if it didn't bother but rather pleased him. "I can hear it now," he said.

"What kind of meat is that, Dad?" I ask now.

"What?"

I point to the meat and shrug.

"Beef."

"Beef?"

"Don't you want any?"

"No, Dad. I don't eat meat anymore. You know that."

I can't tell if he hears this. He stares out the window for a few moments, and says, "I haven't hunted since your mother left."

I nod. I know this already.

"Last year I walked home from the Powwow and came across a circle of men sitting in the field like they sometimes do. They were passing the bottle and talking. It was dark and I couldn't see their faces and I wondered if they were Indians from around here. I sat down with them. One of them said to me, 'I know you. You are the White Hunter. You lost your woman and your heart for the hunt.'"

My father puts several green beans in his mouth and chews.

"Who were they?" I ask.

"What?"

"Locals?"

"No," he says. "The moon was out and when they looked up I could see their faces under their hats and they weren't from here. I don't know how they knew about me, but they did. Then they gave me the bottle and I drank and we sat around for a little while. I said goodnight and came home. It was the oddest thing. It was the first time I felt all right. It was as if the way the man said that, gave me my right place."

"Even if it wasn't a good place?"

"It was the place I belong in the story."

"What story is that?"

"The whole story, the history of the world My part of it. The White Hunter who has lost his woman and his heart for the hunt. That's how I can be told. But maybe I was going to lose faith if I hadn't heard it from somebody sometime." He puts down his fork and looks me straight on for what I think might be the first time since I've gotten back. "Do you know why your mother left me?"

"No."

50

"I got comfortable here and so I got still. And she knew then I was going to be still forever. She knew then I had died."

"Don't say that, Dad."

"What?"

"You're not dead." As I say this, his face turns gray and his eyes go distant and then they close, and his cheeks sink in and the flesh peels away from his forehead and I can see his skull and dirt-colored blood. Then my dad drinks from his glass of juice, and the skin comes back into place. I look at my plate, afraid of what I might I see there, but nothing is out of the ordinary.

"I am still."

"Still is not dead."

"Why did Martina leave you?"

"It's not because I got still," I say. "I can tell you that."

"What, then?"

"I don't know."

"What do you think?"

"Because she didn't believe she knew me."

My father touches me on the shoulder. It is a tender and surprising touch. Then he picks up his fork with that hand and eats a hunk of potato.

"I think it's a good thing you're going to India." He is smiling and I see he has a juice moustache. It makes me feel good about going. I look back on the day and think of the people and places I've seen and the dust of this house and the feel of dryness here and I feel for the first time in a long time absolutely sure of my decision, and of the resulting flight, and of me taking my place in India. "Yes," my father says, "you've got my blessing to go."

"I thought you'd want me to stay."

"I do. More than anything but wanting you to go, I want you stay. Everything will want you to stay. The world itself will conspire against your leaving. Everybody will try to stop you. Your friends will. Your enemies will. You will try to stop yourself. You're likely doing that now. Everybody gets

51

stopped eventually. Everybody gets stilled. And this isn't such a bad place for that. But it doesn't have to be now."

"I've been tired. I was starting to think I needed to stop. That I needed to rest. I was starting to think I couldn't go."

"Some people here, most of the people you know never even went away even one time. When you settle, there you end. As I have. The vital thing dies. And maybe it is a good place and so maybe it is good to stop. You feel like you're done. Like me here."

"Did you always know I wouldn't come back?"

"I understood that you might. I've always coveted your company. I've wanted you back, and I thought you were going to stay the first time, when you visited. You could have gone to the university in Missoula. Do you remember what you told me before you went off to school? You told me that you liked the word 'California'."

"And you told me there was nothing left for me here."

"Was there?"

"I don't know if there ever had been anything. I want to know."

My father nods and drinks from his juice again. "I feel you are still deciding. I saw the phone book, open. You were looking somebody up. Did you find what you were looking for?"

"I found the name, but there was no address."

My father says "There's somebody more you need to see."

"Sometimes I believe I've decided one way or another. Sometimes I'm certain and other times I'm not. Like maybe I won't know until the end."

"Maybe not. Can you get that address?"

"If I really want to."

"If you do, that will be the end? Then you will know?"

"I think so."

We say nothing more about it as we finish eating, but I feel my certainty fading. This seems unfair. At this moment more than any other, I should be sure. In giving me his blessing to go my father has somehow convinced me to reconsider staying. Perhaps this is another trick the me that doesn't want to go—or rather the me that wants to stay—is playing. As I do the dishes, I continue to try to fool myself. I tell myself that I could help my father get the house in order again. I could reconnect with these people I used to know, but in a way more deep than it was before so that I can remain among them. I tell myself that perhaps I could find whatever it was I must have thought I didn't have. I could easily locate Lanada, whatever that would mean. By the time I am done, I don't feel like it's a trick, but a description of a real possibility, one to be seriously weighed.

My father is on the front porch. He watches the highway. The mattress on the glider has disappeared and we sit on it with our backs pressed against the metal bands. My father lights his pipe. "Tell me your story," he says. "You never did."

I don't believe I can tell it. I don't even think I know it. But then I surprise myself by saying, "After we got married it was good for a little while. I thought it was good. We were settled, the new place. But then I began to feel she was unhappy. She asked questions that I couldn't tell why she was asking. But I felt there was an important reason. And I couldn't answer them. She asked me things about myself I thought she knew even though I didn't know them myself. She said sometimes she thought I came from some place of terrible loss. I don't know if she meant an outside or an inside place. I think we were both puzzled by me and what we were together." I'm telling it well; I'm seeing it clearly—maybe for the first time.

My father taps his pipe out against the side of the porch. On the ground below is a pile of ash in various shades of gray, those closer to the bottom being the darkest and those near the top pale. Sediment has hardened into shapes like fossils throughout. He puts his pipe bowl down between us. "Go on."

"By the time Jake came, we knew it was over. I didn't want it to be over. I would look at her in the night. Her face

53

was so smooth and pretty and I could look at it and understand things about who she was. I felt like I could see her heart: And when she spoke I loved the sound of her voice, her accent, and I felt I heard her soul in it. But she saw nothing in my face. She heard nothing in my voice. Only vague things, she said. Only generalities. I don't know why. I felt her missing something. I felt her missing me. By the time Jake was born, we'd already made arrangements. She had to wait three weeks before they could travel. I tried not to get close to her or Jake during that time. I thought many strange thoughts. Sometimes, I thought about killing her. I imagined she had come between me and my baby and if I killed her I could finally pick him up with the love I had for him. I felt that if I killed her I could show him my love. I dreamt almost every night of doing that. But I knew that was wrong. I knew my anger should be at myself. Then she was gone."

My father puts his hand on my shoulder again. I look at the hair on his knuckles and the creases in his face. I think that if I go I will not see him again. I realize that once again I am in the middle of knowing one way or the other.

Now I see I've told the story of me and Martina too neatly. There is something missing in it, some dishonesty in my telling. I realize that I cannot say out loud the depth of the pain I felt. In fact, I have not admitted that pain to myself. I will not tell my father the blackness that opened up within me after Martina and Jake left. The blackness ate at me through that summer and through my final year of school. I can sometime still feel it. Every now and then, I wake up and forget that the entire year has passed and that I am better. I wake and think it is only a few mornings after Martina and Jake left and I feel the blackness. I do not tell this to my father. Nor do I tell him that several weeks after they were gone, I drew long lines down my forearms with a razor while sitting in a bathtub full of warm water and that when I awoke the water was freezing and clouded, and that from that time on the blackness was not as dark and did not appear as frequently.

"Bloodletting," my father says loudly, startling me.

"What, Dad?"

"I saw your arms. I see that you've let blood. You tried to release something. Maybe it worked. Maybe you felt better afterwards. It pains me to see and it worries me, but I understand why you did it and what it did for you. I'm glad you survived whatever you had to where you were. You're done with that place and that time now."

"Did you try to stop Mom when she left?"

"There would have only been one way to do that."

I imagine the crosshairs of the scope of a rifle centered on the outline of a head in a car window. It is my mother in the car. She comes into sharp focus. I can't, though, see my father behind the rifle. This inability to imagine him there relieves me, though I am startled to realize that I can see myself in that place. I think about what my father has said and I want to believe him. I want to believe that one can be done with a place and a time. I want to think that one can live beyond his losses. I want to think that I can go to India and start brand new. Or that I can stay here and begin fresh.

A warm wind with the smell of fires comes off the western hills, which are covered in a haze of smoke. The cars are on the highway in the dusk. My father and I sometimes sat here and played a game where we would each name a color and count cars with those colors to see who got to ten first.

"Blue," I say.

"What?"

I shake my head. A blue car passes. A red truck.

My father says, "I want you to do something."

"What?"

"Lean close to my head."

"What?"

"Lean your head close to my head. Put your ear beside my ear."

"All right."

I do it. I wait for a few moments. Then I sit back. A warm wind passes over us.

"I've always wondered," he said.

"What?"

"If you can hear it from the outside. If you can hear that roaring." He smiles broadly. "Can you?"

"A little," I say. And maybe this is true.

I smile, too. I lean back and look at his face, a good face. I know it is only a trick of light, a trick of the dusk, a trick of the wind; I know it is just a trick of this moment and of the other things that trick, but I feel that my father is wise and has given me wisdom; I feel that neither of us is broken in any way, and that whether I stay or go, things will work, that our worlds are in order, that our stories make sense, and that we are in place within them.

There is nothing in my sleep. I have no thoughts, see no images, and feel no movement. When awake, I feel an impossible amount of time has passed—that I am in the darkness at the end of the world, and it is some mistake that I am conscious in it. All of time has finally passed, and what I've risen to is a place where nothing is supposed to rise again, the ultimate unknown. Then I see the digital clock numbers. I read them and know the real time. It is three in the morning of the day before the day I am supposed to leave for India, three days after the day I left LA, and the third day of my visit to this place I am supposed to call home. I've been asleep for only two hours.

When I sit, I'm overcome with the nausea of fatigue. So I stand up against it. The bed does not know my shape and I do not know the bed. I stumble away from the strangeness of it. The little window on the stairwell is covered and no light comes in, and I move in a sort of panic through the darkness. At the bottom of the stairs is a door I open and go through to stand on the porch.

It is a starry night. Perhaps there was no moon or perhaps it has already fallen. I sit again on the glider, feeling not quite awake. The highway is dead. The street lamps have been broken. Aside from the stars, there isn't a light anywhere, not a window, not a candle, nothing. I have the same sensation

I had before: the world has ended, and this then is a ghost town in which I am alive but should not be. A dog barks at something and his neighbor dog barks at him and I know that I am in the world that has not drawn to a close. Then there are crickets and insects and I wonder if they have just started their noises or if they were only lost to my ears until just now. Against all these sounds, my eyes sharpen. A large white moth flutters around the porch eaves. Then I see that along the other side of the highway, two figures slide through the darkness.

I wonder who they are and what they are doing so late in the night. When I can no longer make them out, I question if I've really seen them. They become visible again and I suppose this proves they are real. I wonder if they are aware of my presence and what they think of it. As I wonder if they feel some kind of anger toward me, it seems to me that both their heads turn in my direction.

"Who are you?" They are too far away to hear me. If they were close enough, I wouldn't ask.

A short and sagging fence stands between them and me, between my father's house and the rest of the world. Of course, it is not just my father's house. It is the house in which our family history has come to rest. It is the culminating point of all the movement of all of those that came before him, and me. It is the point at which everything ends, or at least at which everything up until now can be said to end. I feel the house behind me and its porch over my head and I try to imagine that I am protected by it, and I wonder if that the reverse is true, if I am supposed to protect it.

The figures across the way have moved from my line of sight or have melded into the darkness again. I look at the fence and imagine how easily it can be leapt. I can envision figures like those I've just seen gathering in the long grass on the other side of the fence. I imagine one after another of them springing from the black field into the yard. I can see— it's nothing I have to try to imagine—these figures mounting the porch. Afraid, I slouch, and when this doesn't make me feel invisible enough, I lie all the way down but keep my head up so that I can see. I let my eyes shift from the pines on my left to the fence before me to the open end of the porch on my right and the town beyond. I look it all over again, and again. The smell of smoke is heavy now. I press myself into the glider and watch and smell and hope that whatever dangerous elements circle around in the outer dark will ignore or forget or not notice me.

I stay like this for an indeterminable amount of time. Then I fall asleep, for I dream of flames rising in a circle of blackness until there is only flame. Then they burn away so that once again there is blackness.

I wake very cold.

On my chest lies a heavy hand, which seems to have been extended from beneath the glider. I muffle my cry, as if the owner of the hand may be asleep as well and should not be awoken. Then I try to move away from the hand but my body feels pinned down by it. I remain still for a moment, wondering who is beneath the glider and why his hand is on my chest. I try to push the hand away. It feels against my own hand to be cold and rough and un-reflexive, as if it is the hand of somebody dead. It occurs to me that if I do not get rid of the hand soon, I will become as cold and dead as it. That is when I realize it is my own hand. I realize that my elbow is stuck between the glider seat and its back. Pinched off from blood, my forearm and hand have gone numb. I pry it free and sit up. I try to shake some life back into it and call it back into this world. It takes a moment, but the tingling begins.

Upstairs, I get back to bed but do not sleep. Nor do I stay fully awake. Through the remainder of the night, pictures filter through my mind, of figures and fires, of the faces of people I've known, my own amongst them.

In my half sleep, in my half wake, I wait for the sun.

Before it comes, I know that, of course, I must leave this place where the gray is closer to black, where for every smile there is an image of blood, where the things that still live as if dead and the things that are dead disappear.

But I know also that before I can leave, there are two things I must do.

My mother is surprised I'm at my father's. "What happened to LA?" she asks.

"I graduated."

"I know. I thought you were going to stay out there, put that degree to work. You were with that television studio. You said things were going well. What're you doing back on the reservation?"

I explain that I do intend to use my degree, but in a different way. I tell her about the job in India.

"Teaching Indians how to be Americans?"

"I haven't really thought of it like that," I tell her.

"Whatever made you decide on India, though? Why so far?"

"I'm not sure."

"Maybe it's memories of that girl and the baby you want to get away from."

"That's what everybody keeps telling me, but I don't think that's the reason."

"I guess a lot of time we don't really know our reasons. Maybe they don't even matter."

"Maybe," I say.

My mother and I hardly know what to say to each other on the phone. We talk three or four times a year. Typically we catch each other up with the surfaces of our lives for the first few minutes and then there is some silence and small talk and then it's over. It's as if we became instant strangers when she left; though if I think about it hard enough, I can remember that there was a strain before then. In any case, I was aware before I dialed the phone that this wasn't going to be one of our typical conversations.

My mother says, "When you said that you were back in Montana I worried it was for good."

"For good?"

"Forever."

"I'm pretty sure I'm going."

"Anything is better than staying."

"Please don't say that."

"I'm sorry."

"This place isn't so bad."

"I didn't mean it."

"Yes you did."

My mother says, "It was bad for me."

"Was that it? Was it bad? Wasn't there something more?"

"Well, I didn't just leave the place."

"No. You left Dad."

"Honey, it wasn't working. I loved your dad. I still love him. But we had different expectations of each other than what turned out to be the reality. His world was just sort of winding down into a calm just as mine was starting. I could see that. I don't know that he could."

"Well, he's doing fine now," I say.

"So what has it been, five years or something since you been there?"

"About that much."

"How does it seem to you?"

It is early and I'm by the window in the kitchen. The valley is in a thin layer of smoke, which seems to be drifting down from the northwest and which diffuses the light of the rising sun. I am tired and the night has not cleared from my mind. The smoke descends quickly, as if I'm watching a speeded up video of it.

I say, "It seems like it used to, mostly."

"It's not a place of great change."

I wonder again when exactly I lost my mother. It was before she left; though I don't know how long before. I can think of a time when I had a sense of her as my mother. That was when I was a child and we lived in Colorado. From some distance, I can see her then; I can see us. She walked me to school, holding my hand, and after she released me, she watched me through the fence. It's not a good image I have of her—a blur, like a bad photograph, but it is better than nothing, and despite the fogginess of the image and the memory itself, I can feel a love for me pouring off her. Thinking like this about her now causes a throb in my chest. It is the throb of something lost, the throb I get when I have not prepared myself to think of Martina and Jake but think of them anyway.

During every conversation I have with my mother there is at least one moment in which I find myself trying to see her face. It takes all my concentration. I try first to imagine the lips moving around the words she is saying. I have to remember that she has a wide mouth before I can see it. She has a slight gap in the teeth on her mouth's upper left side, and I have to consciously remember that, too, before it appears. Then I can really see it. I can see the dark, hairless skin around it, the slight pucker and the divot in that swell beneath her nose. I can see the base of her nose itself, the wide nostrils, the way the bridge of it practically disappears into her face. But then I lose it. Perhaps I can conjure her eyes for a flash; they are near black eyes from which you can't tell the pupil from the iris unless you are very close. Perhaps I can conjure a vision of her face as a whole, but I can never hold it in my mind.

I try to think of the things that I feel I've gotten from her. My own eyes are dark as well, but the brown of them you can easily tell from the black. My hair is straight and black like hers. I wonder if there is anything I do or think that is from her—if I have some of her gestures or use some of her words.

"Mom?" I didn't mean to say it. As I hear the word moving into the mouthpiece, it sounds needy and desperate and I suck in as if to catch it before it reaches her.

"What is it, honey?" Her voice is different, too, softer.

"I don't know."

"No?"

This is her voice on the phone. It is all the proof I have of her life. A hummingbird has come into view through the far window. By the time he finishes feeding, her voice will be gone. And then I don't know that I will believe in her. I tell

61

myself quickly the details of her existence. I tell myself about her parents, leaving the reservation in their early thirties, about the way her father dressed and acted like a white man, and how her mother spoke Salish better than English. She had a stroke when my mother was quite young and lost most of her faculty to speak. I remember my mother telling me that she began to feel, as a little girl, that she and her father were legitimately related but that her mother was just a woman who cooked and cleaned in the house. "I lost her young," my mother said of her mother. These are the stories I know of her youth and of her parents. Beyond that: only that they were killed in a car wreck on their way back to the reservation. I wondered often what things they left behind when they moved to Seattle, what lives they might have led had they stayed. All my wondering does nothing to make me know my mother any better.

"Are you there?" my mother asks.

"I hope you are happy where you are, Mom," I say, and in so doing feel almost like the words I am pronouncing are really only one, and that word is goodbye, and I am saying it in a way that will go on forever.

"I hope you are happy, too."

"I will be. I have a lot to do today. People to visit. Dad's driving me to Seattle tomorrow. I have my flight to catch in the evening. I guess I wanted to say goodbye."

"Goodbye," she says.

The drive takes half an hour on a country road that winds past dilapidated farmhouses and fields gone barren. I've been here only once, but I know the way. The road is a single strand, rutted and overgrown at its edges, cutting through a forest of pine. The smell of smoke is stronger now, and I know the fires must be sweeping down and across the reservation. Eventually, there is the Cutfinger place, squat and light blue at the top of a rocky hill, at the base of which I park. Walking up the driveway, I wonder where the road goes beyond here. I can't imagine that it works all the way over the mountain and meets the interstate on the other side, nor can I imagine it curves back round to meet some of the other roads amongst the scattered farmhouses along the highway. It seems this road must just finally end somewhere in the wilderness, that it must grow thinner and thinner, less and less visible, until it just isn't there.

I recognize Bernie Cutfinger's car at the top of the drive. I can see a cat watching me through the window and I remember it from the time I was here, six years ago. I'd started noticing Lanada, who was two years behind me in school, when she became a cheerleader for our wrestling team. During every match, Lanada would break away from the organized cheer and begin to pound the mat with the palms of her hands in an increasing rhythm, and the other girls followed. We talked sometimes in the stands or on the bus. I didn't sit with her during lunch or anything like that, but at some point or another, I began to think that if I could just touch Lanada, my life would feel perfect. Her father, Bernie, had a reputation as a man with violent tendencies, involved from time to time in bar fights in Missoula.

I don't know how I got the courage or the inspiration, but one Saturday afternoon I simply drove to her house. I knocked on the door. Bernie answered. He had his hair in a single braid, and he wore thick glasses that made his eyes seem to glare. I don't remember what I said or exactly how he responded, but he said that I could come in. He called Lanada from out of her room and I can't remember what her face looked like when she saw me there. It must have been surprised. There must have been something else too, some kind of happiness, some kind of hope. Bernie told me to sit at the table and I did. Lanada sat too. Bernie asked me what my plans were. I said I was going to college, probably in Missoula, though the idea of California had occurred to me. I remember thinking that he softened slightly then. He told me that it was wise to go to school and wise to consider one far away. He said the reservation held people too tightly. He said he'd left for the war but that eventually he'd come back but wished he hadn't, and he knew he'd never leave again. I can't remember how long we sat or what we said. Like many of the things I ought to remember, I find it hazy.

After some time, Lanada and I went for a walk in the field, and this part I remember with certainty. It is a memory I like to have. It is a story I like to tell myself. We picked a few crab apples and threw them across the road and into the woods. Then we sat on a rock in the sun and talked. It was spring and I remember a feeling of warmth that day. I remember the soft sounds of insects and birds. I touched her shoulders and I closed my eyes and kissed her. I kissed her for a long time and felt her lips moving against mine. It was as if we were whispering to each other in some very old or very new language, as if these touching parts were telling each other to continue to press so hard that together they would melt, and in melting would pull the rest of us with them and all would be spun and mixed up, so that there would be nothing left of either of us as we had been, or the world as we had known it.

That is how I remember it. There are times when I think on it and doubt my memories, or even the facts themselves. But those are the facts. And if they can be remembered and articulated accurately, can't the rest of it? Can't I put words to the feelings I had and keep them together with the pictures possible for me to evoke? If I see the facts and tell myself the feelings, I can kind of feel them again; they rise and burst in me like bubbles.

I remember I broke the contact, maybe for what I only meant to be a second. It was too late. The whispering had gone silent and I could feel the sun on my back and I could smell the woods. When I looked at her again I felt like I could see past her eyes and I felt like she was seeing past mine. We were the first people, the only people, perfectly united in a perfect place. We knew each other, or almost did. I feel certain of that.

Bernie came down. He took us walking through the pasture. He pointed to the place he'd buried his dog, and told me its name, and said softly that he'd killed it in anger and regretted it. It felt like a good and a terrible thing to know. I admired his confession and his regret, and I believed I'd been given some significant and sacred insight. It felt to me through the course of the afternoon that I'd been accepted into this oasis of a world that existed up here.

I want it to feel like that now, and I realize that I'm here for more than her address, that I needed to see again this place where it all, whatever that is, seemed to be begin.

It is more hot than warm and there is more smoke in the air than pine, but still, I can feel something like what I think I felt back then.

I knock on the door. Bernie opens it looking just as he looked the last time I saw him, in Joe's Station five years ago, about four months after I'd come to his house. It was right before I left for California, and I was with Jason and John, and Bernie gave me only a nod before narrowing his eyes and turning away.

"Hey," he says, as if he's not surprised to see me. Then he steps forward and touches my shoulder. I can't tell from his expression or his touch how he feels about seeing me. He says, "You just show up, don't you?"

I nod.

"Well, nobody's here."

"Just you?"

"Jill's in Missoula, after groceries."

Jill's his wife, Lanada's mother, a woman I've seen but never met.

"I came to see you, Bernie."

"That's a lie."

"It's not a lie."

"I know what you came for."

"What do you think I'm after?"

"Don't say her name. You look for a memory. You look for a ghost. You look for lies." I remember that people are afraid of Bernie. I try not to be afraid. I tell myself my mission is pure and that I will be protected by its purity.

I say "I knew she wasn't here. I came to see you."

I follow him in. The house is well kept and smells good. A big screen television plays a talk show on mute in the living room.

"That's nice."

Bernie looks skeptically at the television. "Was a bitch to get up those steps."

"How have you been?"

"Getting by."

"It's nice here."

"It's shit here, and you know that. Shit in Missoula, too. The bar overrun with a bunch of shit college kids." He takes a Bud Light from the refrigerator and pops the top and hands it to me. "The Indian bars are worse. Filled up with your crowd now and a few old-timers who sit around trying to get free drinks off them. Rez Indians."

I watch him open his own beer and drink from it. I sense in him a loneliness I don't remember sensing before and I feel a darkness rise in my chest.

"There's at least some guys like me left in Missoula, guys who came out of the war. I was only just fifteen, you know that? Viet-fucking-nam. Nobody cares about that anymore. Your bunch is too young. I don't care, either." He shakes his head. On a card table on the opposite side of the room sits a computer with the screen saver flashing blue words.

"Online?" I ask.

Bernie says, "Jill's idea."

"That's why the phone is busy," I say. "I never would have guessed you had it up here."

"Online, the internet, most of it is just shit. They're getting the whole school wired down there with it. Going to give these Indian kids a good electronic education. Learning Without Borders, they call it. My ass. These kids, they're not like you. They're not going to cross borders, go out into the world. Move around the rez, even the white ones. No offense."

"What do you mean no offense?"

He glares at me for a moment then shakes his head.

66

I follow him out the porch where he leans against the railing.

"It's pretty here, that's what I remember. And quiet."

"It's dead."

"No."

"This place is just some purgatory. This is a place for ghosts who haven't moved on, that's all. They're all dead; most of them know it. We're all dead here, just waiting for the liver to die, the car to crash, somebody to pull a trigger."

"Why don't you go?"

"I've been. Now I'm back. Jill, she's the one still itching to move on. But I had my time. I'm too tired. I just stay here and get more angry." He leans on the railing and looks down. He clears his throat, and his voice comes out low. "In seventy-three, me and this fellow I'd served with went to Oregon and got us a logging permit and a truck and started up a business. Those were some times. Just this old pickup always breaking down that he could fix and couple of good chainsaws. We did pretty well. We started thinking of buying a new truck. Started thinking after a year or two we'd buy our own little mill. Cut out the middle guys and be in charge of the whole process, make our own fortune based on our own hard work. But shit, that truck broke down and we tried all afternoon to fix it, and Clooney and me started dipping into our stash of beer. Have a beer, crawl under there and jimmy stuff around. Get out, have another beer. Hell, I don't know what went wrong. That truck, she rolled forward though, right over Clooney's guts. And he comes crawling out all pale—was a pale son of a bitch from the get-go—and smiling like nothing was funny. I was laughing. I didn't know. He says, 'Jesus, that got me pretty good. Maybe we better get me to a hospital.' 'Sure,' I say. 'But how?' The truck was still broke down. We were ten or fifteen miles in. 'Maybe you'd better go for help,' he says. And I seen the blood on his teeth and I seen also that he couldn't stand up. And I knew he was going to die. That he was dying right then. And I opened up his shirt and his guts was turning black, filling up with blood. Jesus, I thought I'd learned a thing in the field, I did my best. I tried to

67

open him with a knife to let out the blood but he'd scream out, 'Jesus, that's hurting me.' He died there. You ever see anybody die?"

"No."

"I seen lots of people die. Everybody I know at all is dead, even the ones breathing."

"I'm sorry, Bernie."

Bernie looks up, but not at me. "It might have been different. Truck rolls or it doesn't. Breaks down or it doesn't. Just happened. I come back here and wished for a long time it could have been different. That we'd bought the new truck we were talking about before that all happened. Or that he'd squeezed a little further under and only gotten his legs broke or something. It could have been that way, but it wasn't."

We stand in silence for a little while, drinking our beers.

"Anyways," he says, "You don't want to hear all about that."

"Yes I do."

"What for?"

"I guess I just like the stories people tell about themselves. It gives me something to hold onto."

"That sounds like bullshit."

"I don't know. Maybe it is."

He looks at me now and I look away. "You're lying to me."

"Yes. I am. I came to see you. That's true. But I want to know."

"What do you think you can know?"

"I feel there is something I need to get here."

"You're just as dumb as the rest of them if you came back here for that."

"I know."

He squares up to me. I am ready for him to lunge. I am not ready to stop him. I am just ready for it to happen.

"I wouldn't get anything into you that way, would I?"

"No."

He shrugs and turns away. "Jill will be back in a little while. You ask her."

"All right, Bernie."

We stand in silence for a while longer. I watch bees in the field and think they are too far from Natural Resources to belong there and so must be wild. I watch ants run around the porch rail. The cat pushes out through the door and walks halfway down the steps before it lies down in a patch of sunlight. From here, I can see the edge of the pasture where Lanada and I sat together on the big rock, though I can't see the rock itself. I try to imagine me and her as we were. I try to imagine us walking together out of the pasture and onto the dirt road. I try to read those faces and know those times. I try to be certain that not only did it happen as I remember it happening but that it felt as I remembered it feeling, and that it meant what I believed it meant.

With his thumb, Bernie presses the head of the ant into the wooden rail. Two segments and several legs are left whole and they squirm.

I say, "Please don't do that."

"It's done." He turns.

I crush the ant.

I follow Bernie back into the house. People move on the television. The computer blinks its blue and its words. The idea that Jill does not live here anymore—that she has left Bernie and he either lies about her returning with groceries or really believes it though it is not true—comes over me.

"What's wrong with you?"

"I'm really tired, Bernie."

"You want to know where she is."

"Yes."

"I've thought of killing that boy she married. Maybe someday I will, even though I know that won't fix her."

I see René DeFrance's face again, and as I think of him I tell myself the same story that I have been telling myself since I first heard that they were together. I tell myself that he is my old nemesis. I imagine that he has stolen Lanada away from me and that with her went things that were rightfully mine.

"I don't know where exactly she is, but Jill, she keeps an address." Bernie walks over to a bureau and opens a drawer. From the drawer, he takes an address book, and from that book, a plain piece of white paper folded several times. On it is written Lanada's Polson address.

He hands it to me.

"Thank you."

"Don't thank me." His head comes toward me quickly as if it means to make contact with mine, but it stops short. "You came up here that one time is all."

"I know it was only one time."

"Sometimes I want to take things and make them what they never were, too. I could even do that right now with you. I could imagine how you could have saved her. But it wasn't like that. There was just that one time."

"I wanted to see her after that. She said there was no point. She said that I was meant to leave the reservation and that she was meant to stay."

"She was right." Having said that, he seems to relax, leaning backward against the table.

"It didn't have to be that way. I could have gone to school in Missoula . . . ."

"You're just trying to make her something she wasn't so you can believe there's a reason to be here. Why do you want to do that? There is nothing for you here. She wasn't for you. Not even that one time. After you left she said it was the strange thing that you'd come. When her mother got home, they laughed about it."

"No, Bernie. There was something there you don't know about." I feel like hitting him and being hit by him as if some sense will come of it. I square myself to him the way he did to me earlier. When I try to glare into his face, I find it is softer than I could have imagined it becoming.

"Tell her something for me," Bernie says.

"Okay."

"Tell her it could have been better."

70

"Okay."

"Never mind. Don't tell her. There's no reason to offer up any lies"

We shake hands. In his face I see all the things that might have been, not just for me, not just for Lanada, or anybody else here, or anybody I've know anywhere, but everybody and everything everywhere. I feel like I see in a flash of seconds all the possibilities of the world—that things can be any way. That there is no such thing as destiny and it all changes. All of history could have been different and all of the future could still be different. We're standing together on a porch at the top of a hill on a reservation in Montana. The mountains are to both sides. The fields are empty, the woods deep. It is late afternoon on a summer day with the Western fires approaching.

We stop shaking hands.

As the only complete north to south route in Western Montana, Highway 24 is usually busy. These are tourists and truckers, moving quickly through the reservation, heading south to Missoula, and north to Kalispell, Whitefish, and Glacier National Park. Travelers are coming in and out of Montana, from and to Canada or Utah or Idaho. Nobody is stopping, not for long. I know only a stretch of the highway, the forty miles between what was once my home and the southern shore of the lake at Polson. I follow the highway out of town and as it winds through a tight valley. I'm driving tired and nervous. Something seems to dart across the road and I swerve to miss it. My front tire spins through gravel and the Jeep jerks, and then by luck, or through some act of instinct, I find I'm driving between the yellow and the white lines again.

A deeper darkness comes over me. This is, I think, a valley of death. I pass the pond where a group of my friends watched Randy Roland became so intertwined in the weeds growing from the bottom that he drowned. I think I see a figure swimming in the shadows there now. When I squint to better see, I find nothing in the water but the dark-topped clusters of weed, ancestors of the ones that drowned Randy Roland, or maybe the very ones themselves. I pass two abandoned gas stations, their windows broken out, fresh and old beer cans and bottles in the dirt lots.

Then there is the small town of Ravalli, from which the highway winds up alongside the hills of the National Buffalo Range. Only a single buffalo is visible, standing in the tall grass on the other side of the fence, his head upheld as if he is looking for something. I wonder why he is alone and I feel for his loneliness. His head cocks and I can see the bowed out bulge of his eye on me.

I reach the top of the incline. The Mission mountains come into view. They are the real wild, jagged and steep, home to glaciers and waterfalls and grizzly bears. Then comes Mission, a faded out town of dust, a town in crumble, where everything is some degree of deterioration except for the mission itself, a tall and wide building of brick and stained glass, standing at the edge of town where it always has, where it stood before the town itself existed. This is where the Jesuits begin to convert the Indians to Christendom and this is where many of the Indians still come for services and to be buried.

I drive straight north now, the Mission mountains five miles to my east. Our first summer in Montana, my father bought a used boat and we made this drive with it to the lake regularly. I felt then as I feel now—that this is not my land, that there are, perhaps, pockets where I belong, but that I am far from them now. The highway is met every few miles by dirt roads cutting through fields, leading to towns I have never known, towns I can't imagine and don't want to. The small farmhouses stand overly somber, absolutely alone.

I am in the heart of the reservation and it gives me a sense of a coming doom, and one that has been.

This is an impossible journey to complete. I shake my head against that doubt, and I think of Lanada's face. I imagine her full and wide lips, her short nose with almost no bridge and its wide nostrils, her black eyes. I'm calling on her for inspiration   and she delivers. I tell   myself that   to pass

72

through such darkness to reach Lanada makes sense. All journeys take on their meaning when the will of the traveler is challenged by obstacles. Now, the smoke has become a haze that lies over everything. There must be a greater fire here, and it must be close, though when I look across the flat land, I can see no leaping flames or plume of smoke to connect ground and sky. It is easy just the same to envision fire running through these fields, across the valley and to the eastern mountains. Without trying, I imagine the orange and roar of it, and the black of it, and the ash.

In the corner of my eye appears the red, ragged blob. It is larger than I've ever seen it, blotting out my peripheral vision to the left. I ignore it. I ignore everything. To go forward one must know that trick, one must keep his eyes forward, his mind as blank as possible. I drive. I pass through the town of Ronan. Several miles outside of it, I see a hitchhiker. He is a short man in a jean jacket and long black hair, his face impassive, his eyes downcast. Even before I finish passing him, I regret not stopping to give him a ride. When he is out of sight, I tell myself that it is possible nobody was really standing along side the road. My eyes have been playing tricks on me. My brain has been addled. I'm in a strange place, externally and internally, and must not take anything at face value. "Forward," I tell myself. "Onward."

Further down, a dog lopes down the side of the highway. As I get closer, I see it is not a dog but a coyote. Again, I tell myself this is likely some figment of my imagination. It is not. I slow the Jeep. The coyote is the skinniest living creature I've ever seen. It turns its head. Its face seems to be covered by a strange halo of light, like an aura. Then I realize it is a series of porcupine quills. They are in the cheeks and tongue and lips and nostrils of the coyote. I pull up beside it and it limps off the road into the ditch. I wonder what to do. I think of my father and the guns with which he used to hunt and how he could perform a clean act of mercy. I think of the hitchhiker and imagine that if I'd picked him up, he'd know what to do. I feel like the only person incapable of doing something right and good for the coyote. It slinks out the far end of the ditch and begins to move east across the field. I tell myself again it is a dream. I tell myself that when one doesn't sleep his dreams seep into waking hours because they must out in some way.

These are lies I am telling myself.

I know that, in fact, I have seen a hitchhiker and a coyote. I know that the man who hitchhikes has suffered before and will do so again. I know that the coyote will die slowly and in pain and that I did nothing about it nor could have.

I go on, through several miles of flatness. Then there is a cherry orchard. The drive is mostly over. I've traveled the length of the reservation almost completely. I've made it.

Coming down through a cut in a hill, I see the lake, its water silver in the light, the bay islands dark shapes. My mind feels to clear slightly and my vision along with it. The red blob is gone. The lake is long and thin—the largest body of fresh water west of the Mississippi. People water-ski here, lie in the sun, play beach games. There is talk of a monster, but nobody is afraid of it. When we went boating, I would often sit on the prow with a towel over my head and neck as protection from the sun, as we cruised past the beautiful homes of rich whites. At dusk, the people would be out in sundresses and sports coats, their dock trails marked every few feet with lights. We could hear them laughing. We could watch them eat and drink on porches and in gazebos. My father waved if he thought we'd caught somebody's eye. Almost nobody waved back. It occurred to me even then that not only were we apart from those white people in their summer houses, but that we were apart from the Indians back home as well, who did not own boats, who did not go to the lake.

I'm descending into Polson. It's still on the reservation, but this is the land Whites began to buy from the Indians right after it had been gotten from the government. I pull over, and from my vantage halfway up the hill, I study the layout of the resort town that is Polson. It is clear where Lanada must live, in a small broken down section to the south. I don't know

74

what this journey will yield but I congratulate myself on making it.

I look again at the water and the horizon.

It is dusk, with the last light flat. I make a wish that it would never get any darker than this.

There is a baby in a blue playpen. He is so still that at first I think he is not alive and that his death accounts for Lanada's flatness, as if she is in a kind of shock. Then I see that he is watching me. His eyes are green, the eyes of René DeFrance. After a moment, they slide from me to the ceiling above my head and away. He wears dirty blue pajamas and has for a companion a faded stuffed elephant. He's a very thin boy, a year and half old, I figure, the age of my own son. He is absolutely silent.

Lanada doesn't acknowledge him. She has given me a can of Budweiser, and we sit together under a lamp, which hangs too low, so that I feel overly illuminated. She wears shorts and a tank top and I stare for a long time at her dark arm and its inoculation scar, something I don't remember, in a place where, when I close my eyes, I only see smooth skin. On her face are dark patches almost like large freckles. There are other differences between who she is and who I remember her to be. There is a chip in one of her front teeth and a lump of flesh below her left ear. Across her forehead are deep lines.

As I start to tell her where I have been and where I think I am going, she nods in the middle of my sentences and stares over my shoulder. I am distracted as well. I glance at the baby from time to time, anxious, for some reason, to know his name.

"He seems very quiet," I say, finally.

She looks around as if she doesn't know what I'm talking about, and then she turns to the playpen. "Babies can be quiet."

"Yes."

Since arriving, I've felt a sense of distance, as if this is a scene in a story I am dreaming up.

"Yes," I say again. "Babies can be quiet."

Then I tell myself this is not a dream, not a story. I tell myself this moment is real. I tell myself that real occurrences have lead up to it, so that this moment is a consequence of those others, and from this moment will come consequences as well. When I think of it like that, I see in a flash the string of things that have lead me here, and the things that have lead to my existence, the history of the world. I see not only the things that have been but the things that will be, all unspooling from this moment, my own future and the future of the world beyond me, the way it will all end.

And then I go blank, as if I've seen nothing.

I sip from my beer.

Lanada turns, and I see in her profile something I think I recognize. Then she turns again and what I've recognized is lost. Still, something hot moves through my stomach. It is a type of excitement and the first deep emotion I've felt since approaching the house. A sense of confidence overcomes me. I can simply tell Lanada to pack and prepare, that she is coming with me to India. Or I can tell her that she is coming back down the reservation and will live with me and my father there. She's given me no signs to suggest that she actually would come on any trip with me, or that if she did come, she could become again who she once was, but I believe it anyway. I believe that she might come, and I believe that what I want to think she once was she can be again.

"Anyways," she says. The corners of her mouth are turned sharply down. It doesn't seem possible that they've always been that way or that they've changed so much since I've been gone. She looks at the door. She says, "René should be home soon."

I look at the baby perfectly still behind the net of his playpen and I look at the TV screen, greengray, and I look at the whitish refrigerator and the stack of dishes beside it and the beer cans on the table. I look at Lanada and see her face as ancient and grim. There is tension in this room that I did not bring but have increased. I feel as if the slightest movement could upset some kind of order. I sip from my beer and tell myself to calm, to maintain confidence in myself and my purpose. Lanada is tapping her foot on the floor, drumming her fingers along the can. Frustration pours off her in waves. The sense of power I had moments ago is quickly fading.

Something in me says that she is not the girl I think she was and that in fact she was never that girl. Something in me begins to say "run."

I know I should follow that advice. I know I should get out. I know I can. I can get up and I can leave. I can say goodbye and get in my Jeep and go to my father's house and wait for the morning and the drive to Seattle and the trip to India. Or perhaps when I wake in the morning it will be with all darkness, even this present black, behind me, and I'll believe I can stay.

Then the front door opens and René is standing there with his light skin and reddish hair and half-slit green eyes. They fall on me and I expect him to give me a look of disgust, but what shows on his face is instead fatigue, as if my presence has drained from him the last of something.

"Hey," I say, trying to smile.

He takes several steps and looks at Lanada. She says my name and adds that René must remember me from the olden days. Her voice is flat. He smiles thinly and nods.

"Yeah, I remember him," he says, coming forward, and offering a cold hand.

"He's up from California for a visit," Lanada says.

"California, huh?"

"I'm sorry to show up without calling or something," I say.

He raises his eyebrows and shrugs. He looks at the cans of beers on the table and then he looks again at Lanada but she does not look back at him. After a moment, René stands for a little while above the baby and then finally leans toward it, putting a hand on the baby's belly. René frowns at Lanada and says, "Has he been fed?"

"Of course."

She opens her second beer.

"He's a mechanic. That's what he does," Lanada says, as he goes into the bedroom. He comes out after a moment and goes into the bathroom and we can hear the shower beating against the curtain.

"That's a good job."

She offers a short, mean laugh. "It keeps him out of the house."

"Well, I had to look you up," I tell her. "It's been all these years and I wanted to see you again."

"Why?"

Perhaps this is an opening I should take, but there seems no way through it. I shrug and drink from my beer. I'm afraid, but I'm not sure of what, of him or her or me.

"You say you saw my dad?" she asks.

My throat is tight. I clear it and say, "He was all alone."

"He's always been alone."

"He had you."

"No."

"And your mother. Now he's got no one."

"She's there."

"I thought she'd left him."

"She's no better than he is. Things don't change like that."

"I'm glad," I say, and I am. It is a relief to be wrong about Bernie and Jill. It almost makes me believe that anything dark or sad I've seen or thought I've seen could likewise be mistaken, false, conjured.

Lanada watches the bathroom door and then gazes into the living room, a blank stare not focused on anything. She picks up her beer and drains it completely. Then she walks to the refrigerator and gets another can and opens it. She walks slowly. Everything about her is slow. I ask myself what could have happened to make her change like this. The shower water goes off. The curtain slides on its rings down the bar. I want to believe René causes this wrongness I sense.

Soon, he'll be coming out here.

I whisper, "Do you remember when I visited you at your house?"

Lanada stares at me for a moment. Her eyes seem to widen. I believe I can see them go back. I imagine she is thinking about that afternoon specifically and those days in general. We are, for a moment, completely connected. I know this feeling—this is the feeling I've yearned for—and I lean toward it. I am about to say something perfect. I don't know what it is, but when I open my mouth it will come. Then I'll know the right thing to do. So will Lanada. We will be saved by what I say and what it means.

Lanada leans away from me. Her forehead goes hard and wrinkled, and she takes a long drink from the beer. If there really was something I might have said, it is gone now.

René comes out of the bathroom wearing sweatpants but no shirt and carrying his jeans and T-shirt beneath an arm. He gives me a quick look and goes into the bedroom. When he comes out he is fully dressed except for that his feet are bare.

"We're almost out of beer," Lanada says.

René looks at me. "It can wait."

Lanada smirks at him and then turns to me. "He doesn't drink liquor, this man. He can't."

René wipes a fall of reddish hair out of his eyes and stares at me, as if I've just insulted him.

"I'm going to the store," Lanada says. She stands and walks to him. They are face to face. It seems like something awful is about to happen between them. Then René steps back, turns, goes into the bedroom and comes back with a set of keys he holds out to her. I see that she is trembling slightly and that the trembling stops when she takes the keys.

"Ten minutes, Lanada."

She starts for the door.

"You heard me, right?"

"All right. Goddamn it."

Then she is gone. René picks up the baby and carries it over to the refrigerator, the door of which he opens. The baby is as still as a doll and he cups its head to keep it from rolling.

René sets the baby down on the counter and I'm glad to see he strike a balance there. René takes out a loaf of bread and some deli meat and a jar of relish.

He lifts up the baby and holds the baby's face close to his own. The baby's eyes do not appear to focus on his father. René frowns deeply and kisses the baby's forehead. "What are you doing, little man? What are you thinking? Good things?" René holds the baby under the armpits and his legs dangle down. They are so thin that I cannot bear to look at them. An urge to take the baby from René comes over me, that urge that blames him for what is wrong with Lanada and what else is wrong here, in this house, maybe beyond it. There is something in me that knows better than that blame, but I ignore that something.

René turns to me. "The gun I keep in that room, it's loaded."

I sip from my beer. It has no taste.

"Do you understand what I'm saying to you?" René asks.

I meet his eyes and am repulsed by the pale of them, the pale of his skin.

He says, "What have you come here for?"

"I wanted to see everybody again."

"There's no everybody. There's nobody here. What did you come here for? You think you know that girl?"

"From way back when," I say.

"She's never mentioned you." He kisses the baby again and pulls him against his chest.

"I used to know her. She was different."

"Different? What does that mean?"

I shake my head.

"You didn't bring answers?" He smiles a bitter smile and puts the baby back in the playpen.

"I'm just looking for my own answers," I say.

"She's a fuck up, a drunk, a beer can whore. That's the girl I married."

I want to stand up, to strike him, to beat him to the ground. Then I realize that I don't really want to do that so much as it is that I'm telling myself I want to.

René sits down across from me. "If you'd married her you could sit around wondering what she'll do the next time she's drunk, who she'll do it with. Yeah? You think you'd like that. And me, I could just go off to California. If I were you."

"If you were me."

He stands up suddenly. "How long ago did she leave."

"About five minutes ago," I say, though I think it has been longer. He looks at a clock, which hangs over a peeling and faded map of the world tacked to the wall.

For a moment, there is more sadness in his face than bitterness. "She has been gone for days before." Then the sadness is gone, and he turns back to me with the corner of one of his lips slightly lifted in what looks like a sneer. "There's nothing to her."

I can hear the truth in some of the things he has said about her. I saw the truth of it in her face before he said anything at all. I try to know the truth so I can move forward from it, but I am not ready. I go back to telling myself that he has grayed and marked her skin, chipped her tooth, distorted her. I go back to telling myself it's not too late for her. Or for me.

"Shit man, it really could be me. This doesn't have to be my life, this fucking circle I live in with her. I know what you want. You want her pussy? No. You want something more." He laughs, looking at me hard. "There is nothing."

We hear a truck pull up. The door opens and closes. Lanada comes in with a case of beer in her arms and a bottle in a bag on top of it. The smell of smoke follows her.

"We've been talking about old times," René says, leaning back.

Lanada puts the case on the counter and unwraps the bottle, a whiskey I don't recognize.

Lanada says to me, "Do you need another beer?"

I want to ignore the truth I've seen. I want to tell her yes. I want to imagine that I can sit and drink beer after beer

81

with her. I want to believe that I will do what she wants me to do. That I will be who she wants me to be. That her face will go slack again and her eyes will reach back and we will connect as we did earlier. I want to think that I will save her in that way, and that in so doing, I will save myself as well. But I know she can't be saved like that, and that I can't either.

"Bring me a glass," René says. "Bring me the bottle."

Lanada laughs quietly and there is something in it beyond the bitterness of her earlier laugher. For a moment, I see what I think is relief on her face.

She puts a beer in front of me. Then she sets down two glasses and the bottle and he pours. René drinks, grimacing. Lanada drinks too, her face filling with bitterness. "He's one of those Indians that can't drink."

As if to prove her wrong, he gulps down what remains in his glass. Then he shakes his head.

"The last time he drank he took a hatchet to the outside of the house. The neighbors called the police. The time before that, he drove his car down to the lake and then pushed it in. We called it in stolen. They knew better, that man from the insurance, but they wrote a check anyway. Just another fucking Indian who can't handle his firewater."

"It's not the Indian in me," he says. "It's the White." His voice is tight. He pours his glass full again.

"It's weak on both sides," she says.

The three of us sit in silence for awhile, drinking. I realize what it is about him I don't like beyond the fact that he is with Lanada and that I am unreasonably holding him responsible for what I see as her fall from grace. What I don't like is that he looks like me. He's as white as I am. In fact, he is me. He is my opposite and my same, and I am disgusted by him and how what he has here means nothing, that in the projection of the life I might have had he has proven it just as worthless.

He looks at me, his eyes watery and strange, and then I see them really focus, studying me, and I realize that in this moment, he's thinking the same thing I've been thinking: I'm somehow him, some version he wish didn't exist, for what it is and for what it isn't.

"Something has to change," one of us says. I check my mouth with my hand as if that will tell me if I've uttered the words. I look at René's mouth. It doesn't move. I feel myself say, "Something's got to give."

René nods. "Change," he says. Then he drinks.

"No such thing as change," Lanada says.

He nods again.

I hear her laugh but it sounds far away. I turn to her and she looks far away, saying. "You think you can make things on the outside change putting the bottle to your lips?"

He doesn't answer but picks up the bottle and drinks from it. His eyes shine, looking like the eyes of a different person, not the eyes that I remember, that I think I know, that I'm sure I hate. I glance around for a reflective surface, something to give me back my own eyes, but there is nothing.

"It will end," René says.

And then I see again relief on her face and I hear the strange laugh from before, the one that is more at ease. It frightens me.

"Fuck you," she says, and when she says it, she seems more sober than she seemed even when I arrived, more alive, more certain.

"Fuck me," he says.

She leans forward. "I don't love you," she says.

"I know."

She laughs again.

He says, "I know what you are doing. Do you know what you're doing?"

"Am I making you mad, René?" It's the first time I've heard her say his name, and it sounds odd.

He grunts. "I know."

She says, "That's not even your baby."

René pauses lifting the bottle from the table. He sets it down and looks at her. "What?"

"Anybody's baby but yours," she says. She jerks her head in my direction. "It's his baby."

He doesn't look at me but lifts the bottle and drinks again.

I turn to the baby. A tremendous pressure has filled my head. I realize it has been building for days. Maybe for weeks. It feels like it will burst and my skull will explode into shards. The red blob appears, hovering off to the side of my head. I understand that the pressure is related to the blob, that one is the product of the other, that they exist only together.

And I realize the baby cannot be mine. This I recognize as the first truly sane moment I've had since coming into this house, maybe since driving through the rez, maybe since arriving here.

"I have to go," I say.

Nobody responds.

I rise and walk past the baby. I walk out the door. The pressure in my head remains, and the red blob comes with me so that I feel blinded in that eye. It's gone cold outside. As I walk through the black, I feel a stronger than normal gravity pull at my feet so that eventually I cannot step again. Then I look back at the house.

I tell myself this is my final temptation. This is the last time I look back and try to pretend there is something behind me that I've missed and can pick up again.

I have to resist the urge to tell myself it's only that she is dead here, and even if she never was what I want to remember he as being, even if us together never meant what I want it to mean, I can still do her good, I can still shake her back to life, and in so doing, I too will be saved.

But now I am confused. I don't know what I think about any of it.

I tell myself that I, too, will find a reason to be somewhere.

I tell myself, What matters is not what was, but what will be.

I tell myself, You can run toward the known and the unknown at the same time.

But I'm not sure what any of that means I should do.

There is the sound of a gun fired. The bullet comes through the front door and clunks against the fender of my Jeep. Somebody yells, though I can't identify the voice as his or hers. Then there is another shot. I haven't moved. Then there is a yell that is his. Another shot rings out. I turn and go back.

Inside, she sits on the couch. Her hands are cupped over her heart and blood runs from under it. There is a small smile on her lips. He stands several feet from the table, rocking back and forth. The hair on one side of his head glistens and red runs down his neck. That eye is dead, but the other eye is open and darts around wildly. It looks at me and then past me to the open door. It looks over to Lanada and back to me. René takes a step with his feet wide. I can see that blood and gobs of matter are splattered on the map of the world. René takes a few heavy steps, raising the handgun and trying to cock its hammer back. His living eye comes back to me as if it means to find something in my face. He gets the hammer back. That shot side of his body slumps. I can smell his wound. He's trying to put the gun to his head again, but his legs buckle. He stumbles toward me and I grab for him. As I clear the gun from his hand, it goes off beside my ear. There is a flash of yellow and a flash of black. Then I feel the release of all the pressure that has been building, as if it is running out through my ear.

For a moment, I think I've been shot, but then I know it isn't true. The sound has caused some explosion in my ear, and that is all.

When I open my eyes René is on the floor.

The red blob is gone.

I scream, and the sound of it is as if I'm underwater. I put the gun on the table. Everything is quiet.

The baby says, "Take me." I hear it through my good ear.

I walk over and look at it, a curl of flesh in dirty blue pajamas. I try to understand how it spoke.

Its mouth opens like a tiny black hole in its face. "Pick me up and take me," it says.

"I will."

I'll take him to India. He is the age of my son. I can have a picture of Jake's passport faxed to me. They are light-haired and light-eyed babies both. No one will know the difference. He will fit right in. To give symmetry to this story—to history, even—I must take and keep the child.

I reach for him. He becomes far away and my arms become long. They stretch toward him. Then my fingers touch his chest.

I hear sirens, far away but getting closer.

And then I know it can't all fall to me. I can't be responsible.

I turn away from him.

"I'm sorry," I say, "but I would never make it with you across the borders I have to cross. I'm sorry, but you are one of those things trying to stop me and I can't let you."

Driving south again, I think about my father. I cannot afford to see him again. I cannot afford to see anybody. I've said goodbye enough. That's all I was here for.

The fires are lighting up the western ridges.

I will keep moving.

My skin is definitely white. I have a reservation for a flight that leaves in fifteen hours. In forty, I will be in a new world, India.

It will be okay there.

§ § §

Fruits of Lebanon

He gradually becomes aware of having awoken. The ceiling, at which he has been staring, is dirty white and high, and the mattress, on which he lies, is so hard as to not seem a mattress at all. He realizes that in a corner of his mind he has been trying and failing for some time to place the heavy, oily odor which hangs in the room.

To one side, he finds a large, open window. Opposite of it, a woman stands in the doorway, shooing an insect he cannot see from her line of vision. He turns back to the window: blue sky and the light green splay of several palms. He looks at the woman again. Her hair is black, her skin dark, eyes slightly bulged. She is slender, though her abdomen looks like a small pillow is stuffed beneath the waistline of her dress. Some strange formation like a knot shows through the fabric there. After a moment, he realizes it must be her bellybutton.

"Hello," the woman says.

He doesn't recognize her. He doesn't recognize this room or what he has seen through its window. Sitting up and seeing his face in the mirror of an inornate bureau against the far wall, he does not even recognize himself fully.

"Be careful," the woman says.

Her accent is unplacable. She smiles and walks toward him.

In the right side of his head is a distant ache, which feels to have its center in his ear.

She extends her hand. "You seem better," she says.

He holds what he finds to be a thin blue blanket against his bare chest with one hand while shaking hers—it is cool and dry—with the other. She doesn't squeeze.

"I'm Ms. Malak."

"Yes?"

"You were very ill when I brought you. You do look better now, without so much color as you had before. It was complicated at the airport, because you were very—*haick*—sick."

"Airport?"

"I met your plane yesterday evening. How did you accomplish your connection in Milan? I suppose somebody must have helped you. In any case, it was difficult to get you through customs. Doctor Sarkis had to be called. His name is important here. We thought then that a rest in your own bed."

"My own bed?"

"Yes, you are welcome."

"I've come through Milan?"

"Yes."

"I've come where?"

"You've come a very long way."

"But customs? Didn't I have to . . . ." He touches his sore ear as if his thoughts can be gathered there.

"Yes, yes, of course. It's all taken care of. In fact, they've already stamped your visa for work. Everything can be done if the proper person approaches it in the proper manner. I've left your visa in the living room on the desk."

Visa. Living room. Desk. He thinks the words but doesn't say them.

"I know you haven't necessarily seen your apartment, but I think you can tell already that you'll very much like it."

She waves again at the insect he still can't see and then she looks through the open window. She says, "You are very lucky to have a place on campus, Doctor. Only the most important faculty stay here. I have been here eight years and they have not accommodated me in such a way. But I bear no bitterness. I understand that we must keep our Americans happy. Of course, you shall find campus still quite empty until vacation ends. We are pleased to see you early so that you may adjust and prepare."

"Adjust and prepare?"

"Yes."

Questions form and burst like little bubbles in his mind. They are incomplete or ungraspable; they are jumbled and fleeting; and further, he has the sense they will not lead him to the deeper question from which he is sure they've risen.

He straightens his back and shifts forward so he can look down from the window. Below, there is a tall stone fence with barbed wire coils running along the top of it. On the other side of the fence is a street overrun with cars and beyond that, blue water bleeding into the sky.

"This apartment affords a lovely view. *Neeyalack*."

"What?"

"Lucky one."

"I don't know that I feel lucky. I don't know what . . . ."

An electric bell sounds from Ms. Malak's direction, maybe even from her body itself, and, for a moment, he is certain he is in a dream. He remembers that for a long time he has been moving through dreams that burn away and replaced by other dreams. He has been spinning with nausea through days and nights and what really seems to be almost the whole of his existence with such dreams, descending only occasionally into the relief of real blackness.

"But I am awake now," he tells himself. And he knows that he has been awake before, that his life has not been all one dream.

The electric bell sounds again.

Ms. Malak takes a cell phone from her handbag and speaks quickly in a language that sounds Germanic, though he knows it isn't. A breeze lifts a stray hair from atop her head and she touches it back into place without appearing to notice its movement or her hand's reaction. He tries again to identify the strong and stifling odor, and again he fails.

After a long moment of silence, Ms. Malak speaks quickly and with apparent passion—perhaps even anger—before clicking the phone off and replacing it in her handbag. She smiles again. He recognizes it as a false smile. Her teeth are large and not quite white, and between all of them are black gaps.

"Your duties begin in one week and a half. We trust you will be well enough recovered by then."

"Duties?"

"Yes, of course, your classes."

There is no question that something has gone wrong. The question is to what degree it has gone wrong. Did he, under the influence of some fever, make some promise or tell some lie? Has he been waylaid? Or has some other mistake—perhaps in identity—been made?

"But I don't understand."

"You will. Dr. Sarkis will meet with you soon—perhaps on the day after tomorrow. He will outline your courses and meeting times. He will show you your office. It is a very nice office. I'm still sharing my office space with two other instructors, but perhaps that will change with time. You have also a new computer. I, in fact, have been waiting for a computer of my own, but you see, I am not an American. Nor am I a doctor. So the best that I can hope for is that the things on which I wait will eventually come to me."

"Yes, but I have no recollection—"

An odd chime—also with electronic undertones—plays a short tune. A perplexed look crosses Ms. Malak's face, and she holds a single finger before her mouth before disappearing from the doorway. Her heels click for ten or so steps. The insect she had been shooing, or another like it, lands on his blanket. It is a mosquito, and the most familiar thing he can find in the room. Ms. Malak can be heard opening a door and saying, "'Allo?"

A voice responds in some way, but what it offers sounds more like a growl than a word.

"Yes?"

Another growl.

"In English. What is it?"

"American?" The word is identifiable but not clear.

"Yes, he is here. But he is not well. He cannot be seen. And who are you to see him? I'll take that but you are not to bother him." Then she speaks several sentences in what he assumes is the language she was speaking before.

90

The door closes. Ms. Malak clicks back down the hallway and appears in the doorway shaking her head over a potted plant.

"Is that the person you told me about, Doctor . . . ."

"Dr. Sarkis?" Ms. Malak grins widely, and, he thinks, oddly. "No, no. Of course not."

She sets the plant as if it is a dirty thing on the bureau. "This is from the boy on the roof. His family and he have lived there since before the war, but they have no legal right to be there now. They make a living watching children and doing wash, but the institution could be rid of them easily and perhaps should."

"The war?"

"It's not the proper word and I shouldn't have used it. In certain company, it is referred to as the incidents. But then, you are not certain company. You have your own war now, but I assume that you call that what it is."

He nods his head, but he is still uncertain as to what wars or incidents she is referring.

"Some say all our past events are waiting for the right time to repeat themselves. But it is important one not think in that way, or else how does one go on? It was an awful time. Your own Marines were here until the bombing of the embassy. Then they left. Everybody knew it was the time to leave then. The ships were pulling out to sea, the helicopters were lifting into the air, and they were gone."

It is all vaguely familiar but not completely graspable. "It was a civil war?"

She laughs. "They called our war a civil war, but what war is civil? In any case, all that is supposed to be over. Those times are supposed to have past. The Christians and the Muslims live side by side in the way they lived before. They have something they are calling peace at the border. If only things do not get out of control where your troops have now gone then perhaps there is hope." she motions in a specific direction and he watches her hand as if it will help him understand what she is saying. "In any case, in this country, at this time, it is as it was before. The Americans are welcome

91

again. They are wanted here." She smiles more broadly and more falsely than before.

He realizes that she hates him.

"I suppose that is what everybody wants," he says. "To be wanted, I mean."

Her eyebrows rise and then narrow together over the bridge of her nose. After a moment, she says, "Yes, to be wanted. Let us hope the cycle has been broken. Let us hope that your most recent problems don't result in it all beginning again, so that the Americans who are so wanted don't feel themselves again . . . unwanted."

She looks out the window, her face pensive. Then she lowers her eyes to him and says, "In any case, you brought very little. Dr. Sarkis has been gracious enough to draw some money through the Institute. I have sent your clothes to be laundered and,"she points to a box on the dresser, "have taken the liberty of buying you two pairs of pants, two shirts, several pairs of socks and other underlying essentials. It seems you left the States in some sort of disarray, or perhaps your luggage has been misplaced. I have ordered groceries and they are in your refrigerator and cupboards."

He is struck by the truth of her statement that he left the States in disarray. Nothing specific comes to mind but he squeezes his eyes closed against a pain that moves through his head. He utters a question that seems to come from nowhere: "Do I like myself?"

"What?"

"Nothing. I was wondering about the apartment."

"We make it as comfortable here for you as possible."

"Where exactly is here?"

"Beirut, Doctor. The American Institute of English Language. The most respected training ground for English language in all the Middle East, maybe all the East. This is the place, Doctor, where the best learn."

He doesn't know what he is, exactly, but he is certain he lacks the credentials with which she seems to be crediting him. "No, I'm no doctor. I'm sorry. I think maybe a mistake."

"Ah, well. Never mind about that. We are sure your intentions are good."

"But I don't have any intentions."

"In any case, here you are." She motions around with hands flattened toward the ceiling. "A very beautiful place. How can you expect to be anything but happy, Doctor?"

"But what I'm saying is even though I've been to college, I'm sure I haven't gotten a Ph.D. Those duties that you mentioned, if they have—"

"It is better anyway that you continue to let us think otherwise." The lid falls heavily over the bulge of her left eye and then rises slowly. "You are not a man above a little dishonesty, are you?"

"I really don't know."

"You're here, Doctor."

"But to what end?"

She raises her eyebrows. "Doctor, please, you are still not fully well."

"Yes, but—"

"It is best for you to sleep."

"You said I have duties? You say I have a job?"

"Of course. I said both of those things."

"May I see my contract?"

A look of sternness crosses her face, and then it softens as she stares through the window again. "Yes, yes, of course. In due time."

"You see, I can't remember much."

"Perhaps you don't want to."

Images flash through his mind. A figure on a street. A car passing. A living room with bright light coming into it. A grassy hillside. A palm tree. The face of a woman in near darkness. Two small children walking hand in hand down a sidewalk. A bicycle leaning against a wall. He does not know if these are memories of things from his life, or if they are memories from films he has seen, or if they are perhaps images from books he has read; he does not know if they are dreams or simply products of his now awaken imagination.

"From where you've come hardly matters, does it, Doctor? Here you are. I imagine you've come for a fresh start, for I can think of no other reason. You must get well."

He wonders after the sickness from which he is emerging, and the fogginess of his memory. The idea that she has given him some kind of drug to induce these things passes through his mind. He finds he has no real desire to confront her with such an accusation. He wonders briefly after his own nature, if this kind of lapse in assertiveness is typical of him.

"In any case, I've been speaking too freely before you."

"I need you to speak freely to me."

"I have to tell you about something amusing, Doctor. You look as if you could be Lebanese, which, I think, will disappoint Sha…Dr. Sarkis." She chuckles and adds, "You see, he spent a year in Texas. I think he was expecting somebody obviously American. We're a strange place, Doctor. Half of the Lebanese love Americans. I don't know if it is really love. Anyway, we think we need Americans. And Dr. Sarkis wants you to be American, because now—"

"But I am American."

"Yes. But not as they are in Texas, I think. No, decidedly not. Not from what he describes of Texas, not from his photographs. He can even speak like a Texan if he wants, but it is unlike the way you speak."

"I'm not from the South," he says.

"In any case, they've … we've … made things nice for you. I've put two hundred thousand in a drawer in the kitchen. It will, of course, be deducted from your first month's salary, but it is very gracious of them to offer such an advance, along with the clothes and the groceries, of course. You will find there also what little American money you had in your pocket as well as a few other things. Your watch, for example. Your passport, naturally, is at the Office of Human Resources. They shall need it for some time. I must be leaving you now. Here is my card with my cell phone number included. Please do not hesitate to call me. You are in my charge. But for now, sleep, rest, get fully well. *Ciao.*"

94

She puts the card on the bureau a good distance away from the plant. Then her heels click down the hallway.

"Good-bye," he says.

The apartment has two bedrooms and a large bathroom with a tub. There is a living room which opens to a balcony, on which sit three stone potters full of dry soil. The balcony overlooks the fence with its coiled wire and the busy street and the sea beyond. There is a small kitchen. The floors are made of stone tile, which are cool against his feet, despite the heat, which wafts through the apartment. Scattered throughout it are various pieces of furniture: a couch and matching arm chair, a round table, six matching dining chairs, two bureaus—one in his bedroom and one in the living room—two beds, a coffee table, and several end tables. Upon close inspection, he realizes all the furniture has been much used but recently polished and otherwise cleaned to make look new. The arm of the couch, when pressed, gives way so that he can see the series of staples meant to hold it to the frame. Opening a door of a cupboard in the kitchen causes it to fall off. In the hallway between his room and the living room are long black streaks as if somebody has dragged dirty fingers there.

It appears he is on the sixth or seventh floor. From the window opposite of those facing the balcony he can see a tall, modern looking building with huge terraces, most of which are shaded by red and white striped awnings. He sees no sign of life in the building.

Between his balcony and the sea there is only a small empty parking lot, the fence, the busy street—it appears to be two lanes wide but it accommodates four lanes of traffic—and a strip of sidewalk along which people—too far away to tell anything about—walk.

"Beirut," he tells himself. "This is Beirut." It sounds exotic and the idea that he is actually in it is vaguely exciting. He wonders again if he meant to come here and is instantly certain that he did not. He is just as certain that he did mean to go somewhere and that he was leaving the States for a reason.

A sharp pain moves though his head again. He touches his ear, which aches vaguely. A sort of anxiousness haunts him so that he wants to keep moving. He goes back into the kitchen and tries to put the door back on the cupboard but the wood into which the screw is supposed to turn is too tattered. Throwing up his hands, he wanders down the hallway and stops in the bathroom to study his face, which has become more familiar. Now certain near-memories occur to him and he feels that if he sits down and concentrates he may be able to drag out something substantial, but the idea of it overwhelms him, and he decides that a continued exploration of his apartment will be a better, or at least a safer, use of his time.

He finds blue and yellow bills in a kitchen drawer and puts them in his pocket, leaving the twenty-five dollars in American money behind. When turned, the water taps do not produce water. Suddenly he feels the urge to bathe. He finds a three-gallon bottle in the pantry and pours it into the bathtub. Somebody has left a small sliver of soap, which disappears in his hands halfway through his washing. He sits on the edge of the tub to dry. After dressing in the clothes that are now his and fit him well enough, he opens the main door and looks above it to see he is in apartment 603.

"603," he says into the emptiness. There is an elevator halfway between his door and the one at the other end of the hallway. Hanging by itself from a nail beside the door is a key, which he tries in the handle; it works. He puts the key in his pocket and steps outside of the apartment.

On the elevator door hangs a piece of paper which reads: "Due to the unfortunate over-consumption of water by those living in this faculty building, we have regretfully been forced to make the decision to cut off water supplies between 10am and 6pm each day. This decision will stand until further notice is given. Kindest regards, Physical Plant."

"But that woman told me nobody was here," he says to the piece of paper. "How could they use up the water if they are not here?"

The elevator works and he goes down. Outside is the nearly empty parking lot, at the entrance of which sits a blue clad guard with head hung down as if bored or angry. The street he saw from above is indeed busy; cars honk and speed past. It is very hot.

"Beirut," he says.

He turns away from the traffic and back toward the building from which he has come. A figure darts across the building entrance. He stares into the black space wondering if he has been victim of a hallucination. Then a dark, shaggy head with deep set eyes and thick eyebrows peeks out. Finally, a lanky boy—perhaps young man—steps into view and gives a quick, short wave. He waves back. The boy, whose large head hangs to one side, smiles deeply and points upward.

He nods as if he understands; though he does not. Then the boy is gone.

To the left of the taller, newer looking building which faces his, is a set of stone steps leading up a hillside thick with foliage. Buildings sit in pockets amongst the green. He notes, as he ascends the stairs, at least a dozen cats. They are of all sizes, lounging in the sun, in the shade, sniffing around. At the top of the stairs, buildings, including one which is home to a tall clock tower—four o'clock, he notes—are clustered together. These buildings are hemmed in by the same sort of stone fence and coiled barbed wire he saw below. It occurs to him that maybe he should not pass through such a daunting barrier, but he feels that his choice is between exploring his new environment or sitting and pondering the most obvious questions about whom he really is and from where he has come and why.

Walking along the fence, he finds a small exit and before it another guard, who peers at him with caution. Slowly, a smile grows beneath the man's mustache.

"'Allo, Doctor," the guard greets him. "You are as Malak says."

"Hello," he says. "What do you mean, I'm as Malak says?"

"You're not so American, Doctor?"

"I'm from America."

"From the States?"

"Yes, from the States."

The guard grins at him. "Maybe it is better sometimes not to look American."

"Can I go through here?"

"I am not here to stop you, Doctor."

"Who are you here to stop?"

The guard smiles as if he feels the question has been in jest.

He passes the guard and goes through the little archway.

This street, too, is packed with cars, and they give the same impression of disorder he got from the street below. On the other side, people walk past or stand in front of mostly open-fronted shops selling food items and other shops with large glass windows displaying shoes, books, computer equipment. Several of the buildings along the street appear new, while others appear ready to collapse. Between the new and the old buildings stand half-completed edifices.

He crosses the busy street with some difficulty. Almost all of the shop signs are in English and Arabic, or even English alone. The women are well dressed, with perfectly made up faces, though, by and large, the men are in more casual clothes. Shades of skin vary greatly; so, too, do shades of eye and hair color. Nobody looks what he considers to be very Arabian, though when he hears them speak, it is in what he assumes to be Arabic. Everybody seems rushed. Many people are talking on cell phones as they walk.

He places everything he notes about the people and the setting firmly in his mind as if it the details are things he will need to hold. A fear that his desire to make meaning out of his immediate surroundings will put more distance between himself and the place he was supposed to be passes over him. This causes him to wonder if there really is a place that he is supposed to be. It's not the place that he left—for of the necessity of that leaving he is certain—but there may be a place, just the same, he intended to go and has not reached.

He walks. The smell he noted earlier is stronger here, and he identifies its source, or at least a portion of it, as a large steel pot, which seems to be simmering in the entrance of a shop. The scent is more concentrated here but oddly less bothersome. Perhaps, he is getting used to it. He turns the corner. This street is narrow and less busy. Now the shops are more like five-and-dimes in the States. There is still a mixture of old and new, of decay and brightness, and amongst it more buildings which have been what he assumes abandoned during the skeleton process of their formation.

It is impossible not to be aware of the heat, and yet he feels that its power comes on him all of a sudden, so that he finds himself standing still on the sidewalk, his mouth slightly open, looking, he thinks, the way a lizard on a wall looks. Where he has gotten this image quickly comes to him. It is something he saw in Mexico. He remembers, in a general way, that he has traveled there. In fact, the overall mass of his life has a shape in his mind. It is shadowed in places, and he knows lighting those areas would require a force of effort. He is confident that if he applies that force, the details of most everything, at least everything but the trip here, will bloom back into his conscious mind. He does not really want to make the effort. He wonders why. He wonders if he has hidden things about what he has done and who he is from himself on purpose.

His ear throbs.

He turns his head slowly to the side and sees black and white curtains hanging over several large windows and a sign which reads: Internet Café.

Inside, it is cool and smoky. There is a small bar and behind it a smiling man in a burgundy shirt. All around the bar are tables, and at each table, a computer, and in front of each computer, at least one person, though many tables contain two or three people.

A pretty girl of nineteen or twenty—he thinks of his own age, twenty eight, something of which he is certain—with her black hair pulled back, and a small, delicate face, approaches him. She is dressed in a thin, low-cut blouse, which reveals the cleavage of breasts large for a girl so thin. Above each eyelid she wears a whitish smear.

"*Mahabah.*"

"Hello," he says.

Her smile reveals small, bright teeth. "Hello. Do you speak Arabic?"

"Not at all."

"*Mahabah* is like hello. Do you want me to sign you in? There is a computer upstairs still." Her accent causes the end of each word she speaks to lilt.

"Sign me in?"

"To the internet."

She studies him as if slightly perplexed. He doesn't know what to say.

"You're from America?"

"Yes."

"You can call them there. It is too cheap through the internet. It is next to zero."

"I didn't come for calling. It was hot. I'm just trying to get my bearings."

"Bearings?"

"Yes, to know where I am. I haven't been here long."

"Ah, bearings. I am Manal," she says.

He takes her hand. It is warm and firm.

"I am happy to meet you. My English is not perhaps too good, but I am French-educated," she says, shrugging.

He glances again at the cut of the girl's dress and the cleavage she has exposed. A surprising sensation of lust comes over him. He wonders if he is a typically lustful person. Maybe it is not lust, he thinks. Maybe it is only loneliness disguised.

"Would you like the computer?"

"All right."

"*Yella.*"

He follows her high-heeled shoes, her nylon-covered legs, her black clad buttocks, up a series of steps. His desire for her grows. He tries without much effort to think of the last woman he touched, held, kissed, made love to. Something distant begins to surface, but a panic overcomes him and he rejects whatever it is trying to work its way into a clear place in his mind.

"Do you like it?"

"The café?"

"Beirut."

"I think so."

They are at the top of the stairs. The loft is dim and overlooks half of the café. All the girls look pretty to him. Manal is smiling.

"Do you have an email account?"

"I think so. But I can't remember it."

He sits on a padded bench, and she leans in front of him to click her fingers across the keyboard.

"This is my account."

"You don't have to do that…"

"No, no. Never mind. It's only an email account. We have to use it to get on to call. It is impossible without."

"It's cheap?"

"Five thousand an hour. Two dollars."

"Okay."

"Type in the number and you will call."

He thanks her and watches her go down the steps. Then he stares at the screen. He supposes if he thinks hard about it, he can come up with a name and number to call, but to what ends he does not know. It occurs to him to call a number randomly. He thinks of an area code: 323, Los Angeles. Using the keypad, he dials it and then seven other numbers he lets his fingers choose. The headphones make a strange buzzing sound. Then there is a ring.

He half expects his hands have pecked out some number he should be calling. He wonders if he will recognize the voice that responds, and that in talking with the person to whom the voice belongs he will solve all of the mysteries concerning where he has been and where he was going and why he is where he is. The voice that answers, however, is unfamiliar. It is a man's voice.

"Hello?"

"Hi."

"Yeah, what? It's seven o'clock."

"I just called to say, 'Hi.'"

"Who is this?"

"I just called to see how you are doing."

"Yeah, okay, but who is this?"

"You don't know?"

"Yeah, I don't know."

"Well I guess you're fine. Except that you don't know who I am."

"Am I supposed to know?"

"Don't you think you are supposed to know?"

"Listen puckerhead, if I knew I wouldn't ask you. If you're calling up to be funny you can flip off."

"I wanted to know about your refrigerator . . . ."

"What the heck?"

"If it's running."

"Did Mark call you or something?"

"Perhaps it was Mark. Is your refrigerator running?"

"Yeah, of course . . . ."

"Well you'd better stop it before it gets away."

There is a silence. Then: "Who the flip is this?"

"You know."

"Yeah? Maybe I ought to kick your butt."

"Maybe you ought to try to kick my ass."

"Okay, I'm definitely going to kick your butt now."

"My ass? I don't think so."

"Mother flipper, are you kidding me?"

The sense that he cannot keep this going any longer causes him to pause. He wonders how he kept it going so long. He has the impression that the urge to call and joke like this is not really natural to him. Despite this feeling, he hears himself say, "I know who you are. And maybe *I* ought to kick *your* ass."

"All right you puckerhead. You know who I am, then you know where I am."

"That's right. I know where you are."

"Well why don't get your tail over here right now and we'll see who kicks whose butt."

"Whose ass?"

"Your flipping butt you flipping puckerhead. You better get over here."

"Okay."

"I'm going to hang up the phone. And then I'm going outside to wait for you."

"I'll be right there. I'm not far away. Go ahead and go outside and wait. Then I'm going to come by and kick *your* ass."

The phone clicks off.

He is not sure how he feels about what he has done. He pictures a young man curling and uncurling his fists, looking up and down the street. This causes him to giggle. Then the giggling dies away. The scene he imagines becomes one not of farce, but of frustration. The face he has created for the young man twists in anger, and small teeth grind together behind dried out lips. He takes off the headphone and gets up and goes downstairs to find Manal.

"Did you sign off?"

"No, I didn't know how."

"I'll do it. Did you call your family?"

"Sort of. A guy I know, Mark."

He takes money from his pocket and she counts out of it three blue bills. Then she says, "If you need my help, here is my cell phone number. I can show you all the places to go. And I can help so the people don't take advantage of you. Many of them will have a motive with you."

She hands him a piece of paper with her name and number written on it.

A simple sense of sadness has come over him and as he looks at her and then down at her carefully printed number, it increases. He feels like apologizing to Manal, perhaps because she used her account to sign him on and he did something silly and maybe even cruel with the call. Now he wonders if he is a cruel person, or if he is a sad one, if either defines his nature.

Hungry, he finds a small restaurant with two workers in green caps and aprons. There are no other customers. The men are watching a small television that sits on the food counter. He orders the only Middle Eastern food he knows: falafel and hummus. The hummus is delivered quickly, under a ring of olive oil with chickpeas in its center. The falafel come a moment later, darker and harder and smaller than the ones he has had before. The smell of the city is on the food, but putting a bite of hummus into his mouth, he finds it good.

Chewing, he thinks that if he tries, he can get completely used to the odor.

Swallowing, he considers the idea that food makes all people the same.

Dipping a falafel in hummus, he decides that what he really means is that hunger, not food, makes people the same.

He considers this inner-discussion as proof of a philosophical side to himself and it is a pleasant discovery. He considers the fact that he has eaten and he has a bed to return to. These are good, simple things. Perhaps he was in search of simplicity. Perhaps, if that was, indeed, what he sought, he has found it, even if by accident.

He tries to greet with his eyes and his smile people that pass by on the other side of the glass, though nobody seems to catch this greeting in time to respond. He nods and chews and smiles just the same. After a while, his guts let out a groan that indicates he has had more to eat than he should have. The food has left an aftertaste that grows increasingly disagreeable. The idea of needing to get used to certain things—smells, foods, people—is now daunting. He looks out again at the narrow street and the people passing and doesn't feel the same kinship he just did with them.

He leaves a bill on the table and ventures out. It is dusk. The street is busier than earlier. Cars and mopeds zip by. Taxis honk, and he understands they are asking if he needs a ride. He shakes his head. After he has gone a block, he notes that two men, each short and dark, are walking at his pace on the sidewalk across from him. When he stops and looks at them straight on, they stop as well. They lean toward each other and talk. One of them seems to glance over.

104

He starts walking at a quicker clip. The men across from him start walking again but don't go as fast as he is going. Still, he is sure that he is followed. Not far down the street is a narrow doorway edged in stone. The words "Rock Inn Night Club" hang on a sign above it. He pushes the door open and ducks through it to find himself in the midst of fifteen or so women. Many of them appear pale and several are dancing together while the others sit at various tables or along the wall watching. It is a dim place and smoky. A few men in groups of two or three are scattered at tables close to the dance floor or sit along the bar. Behind the bar are three women dressed in seemingly identical black slacks and low cut tank tops that are also black.

He sits down at an angle so that he can face the door and see if the men on the street followed him. The barmaid closest to him is plump, with long blond hair and a bulbous nose. She rises and leans forward.

"Hello," he says, "how are you?"

"I'm nice. What would you like to drink?"

"A vodka tonic," he remembers.

"A what?"

The men along the bar are watching him with stern faces. He looks from them to the door, which, to his relief, still does not open. He thinks of the wall and the barbed wire and wishes he were behind it. He nods to one of the men. The man nods back. The barmaid asks him again what drink he ordered.

"Vodka tonic," he says. "Just vodka and tonic water."

"Okay." She yells something into the kitchen, perhaps in English, perhaps in Arabic, perhaps in some other language. Then she turns and smiles at him. A hand appears from the kitchen. It is holding a large clear glass that is handed from one black clad woman to the other and then to the one that greeted him. She puts it on the bar before him. It is almost pure vodka and the water is not tonic. He wonders if they have used bottled water and if not, if the alcohol will kill anything bad for him in the tap water.

"Will you invite me to join you?" the barmaid asks.

"Okay," he says, and as he does, that he is in a brothel dawns on him. She pours herself a tall beer with a thick head and drinks of it.

"Cigarette?"

"No thanks."

"Do you have a cigarette?"

"Sorry."

"It's okay."

"Where you are from?"

"The States," he says.

"I'm from Romania," she says.

In the mirror behind the bar he can see the flash of blue and red lights. He can see limbs and fabric swaying out of time with the music, which, although unidentifiable to him, must be Arabic. The other two women behind the bar glance from him to the dance floor and back to him. They look bored.

"Are these your sisters?"

She seems to think for a moment as if deciding what the best answer is. "Yes," she says. "My two sisters."

He nods.

"We live all together in one room."

"One room only?"

"Beirut is a very expensive place. But we must come here for money."

"Are all these girls from Bulgaria?"

"Romania. We are from Romania."

"Are all these girls from Romania, or just you and your sisters?"

She looks around, her eyes widening a little. They are pretty eyes, moist looking, and clear. "No. Other places. Bulgaria. Russia. Kazakhstan"—she points to girls on the dance floor as she says the places—"everywhere."

"Do they—do you—make very much money?"

She shrugs. "Enough to have the roof, to eat." She rolls a shoulder to a slight man sitting at the far edge of the bar where there are no lights. "He makes very much money. But if he is happy, he is good to us more. We make him happy more by doing good, and he is good to us more."

"What is good?"

"Money is good."

He nods. He says, "Do you miss your home?"

She shrugs. "Of course. Everybody misses his home. But we have to do it what we do, to make money, to live. I miss a place where there was no money and no way to live. All of us are like that. Why else would we go from there? Why else would we come here? Why does anybody leave the place that is his?"

"Yes. Those are good questions."

"Why do you come here?"

He sips from his vodka and turns to look at all the pale girls in their short skirts dancing poorly and—it occurs to him now—sadly, though some of them smile. He looks at the men scattered and smiling hungrily. In the corner on the opposite side of the dance floor a man and a woman sit together talking. He turns back to the barmaid.

"Why did you come here?" she asks again.

"To this bar?"

"To this country."

He sips of his vodka. "I don't know," he answers.

"Everybody knows."

"I don't."

"Maybe you do."

"I don't think so."

"Maybe you do but don't want to tell it. Or maybe you inside your heart don't want to know."

"I must have had a reason. Maybe I wanted to shed my skin, whoever I was."

He glances over the entire scene again and then one more time. Then he looks back to the barmaid. She is now nodding slowly, keeping her eyes on him as she lifts the beer and tips it to her mouth. When she puts the glass down, foam is on her lip. Her throat seems to tremble from the swallowing, and her eyes are wider.

He is overcome with a sudden urge to help her. Exactly why he thinks she needs help or how exactly he can help her is ambiguous to him. In fact, it seems quite unlikely that he could help her at all. This desire and his helplessness in accordance with it stretch back now through the day and the people he has encountered in it, as if they all have some under-identified need and he wishes he had some unidentified answer for it.

He drinks from his vodka again. It burns his tongue and it burns his throat.

"Are you lonely?" the barmaid asks.

"I don't know."

"I can go with you in only two hours."

Despite its heft, he finds the pale and smooth of her flesh pretty. "Luxurious, even," he says quietly. He can imagine himself alone with her. He can imagine touching her. He glances at the bar. Her beer is empty. She is waiting for him to answer. He imagines a woman—not the one before him, not any woman he has seen in this brothel or even in this country—stepping nude from a shower. It is some woman with whom he is familiar, though before he can identify who exactly she is, her face morphs into Manal's. She stands nude for only a moment before her flesh begins to expand and takes on the shape of the barmaid before him.

His head hurts. He shakes it slightly against the pain. He wonders whether it is hunger, which really defines him or sympathy. He wonders whether he wants to help the women of whom he is thinking, or if he really wants to have them.

"Shall we, you and I, make an arrangement?"

He says. "I should go home now. Maybe I'll come back again."

"The drinks are very expensive here," she says, taking several bills from the roll he presents her. He nods. He leaves another bill on the bar.

The vodka feels heavy in his stomach. Surprisingly lucid just the same, he walks, knowing, by accident or by instinct, where to turn. When he reaches the Institute wall he follows it to the gate. A new guard there studies him skeptically and speaks to him in Arabic. He shrugs his shoulders and the guard addresses him in English. "Are you the American?"

"Yes."

The guard's eyes still show skepticism. Then: "Okay, okay. Go ahead."

Bats flitter in the light of a street lamp diving after insects into the darkness beneath the wide-reaching branches of a tree. Cats roam. Some stop to study him, and a few follow him. By a fountain close to the top of the steps sits a kitten, its paws curled beneath it, its eyes gummed shut. It mews. He lifts it by the nape of the neck. It mews again. All of its bones seem to be visible. There is a movement in his guts he refuses to consider. A passing cat glances at him. A bat comes flitting by.

Holding the kitten to his chest, he walks down the steps and to his building. He takes the elevator up and pauses only for a moment outside his door, uncertain of the idea that it is actually his. The key fits.

His shirt, sweated through, hangs on a chair. He has cleaned the kitten's eyes with a paper towel. It looks at him now as he pours milk from a bottle and spoons tuna fish from a can onto separate paper plates. Then he sits back and watches. The kitten pays no attention to either of the paper plates. Instead, it takes several steps toward him.

He turns it around and pushes its head toward the milk. At first, it seems to resist but then has nothing with which to offer resistance. Its nose sinks into the milk. He releases the kitten. It lifts and shakes its head, and then it turns to look at him. Being as gentle as he can, he forces the kitten's head close to the tuna, but it only steps back and tries to shake the oil from its whiskers.

"What then?"

It steps toward him.

He pushes it back toward the tuna and the milk.

It turns and starts toward him again.

He rises and walks to the other side of the room. "Forget me," he says. "Eat. Drink." The kitten stands with its legs splayed and its eyes slit. After a moment, it sits.

He goes down the dark hallway and into the dark bathroom and washes his hands. When he returns to the living room, he finds the kitten standing beside the chair and mewing to the shirttails as they move in a breeze coming through the open balcony door.

"Don't you know you need these things? Don't you care?"

The kitten looks toward him. Its eyes are blue and milky. He picks the kitten up and takes it to his bed. He undresses and gets beneath the blanket, putting the kitten on his chest, where it sleeps, purring for a short while and then goes quiet. He himself drifts fairly quickly into sleep. He dreams with an exaggerated sense of this afternoon and evening's hunger for Manal, and the barmaid, and other women from the brothel, as if he wants to eat them all. Or, perhaps it is the reverse, that he would like them to feed on him, for what he sees in his dreams is them kneeling to the side of him, faces buried in his body, as if they are in some act of devouring.

Later that night, he wakes to an explosion, and then a series of them. There are loud and deep voices. He sits up, squeezing the kitten against his chest. The history of the country in which he is living comes back to him. There are men below with guns, meaning to kill each other, to kill themselves, to kill everybody. Terrorists planting bombs. Bombs falling from Israeli aircraft and shot from Israeli guns across the border. Perhaps as a consequence of the war in Iraq, the war between the nations has resumed. The civil war here has rebloomed. The hatred has resurfaced. Militias have organized in secret and are coming into the dark bearing arms. The line toward the center of the city has been drawn again, Muslims to the one side, Christians to the other. They are torturing in the tower again. Syrians soldiers are flooding the streets to fortify against the Israelis. Some of the militias are siding with the Syrians, some are siding with the Israelis; some are siding with neither, and some are siding with both. The

Israelis are going to leave the city in ashes once and for all. The world is chaos.

At first, the prospect both excites and calms him. These are the final moments. The explosions continue. The sounds of voices grow more strained. It is Armageddon, at last, the ultimate relief. Certainly soon he will hear a loud whistle, and the whistle will become the blare of a horn. Then there will be darkness. But there is the kitten, cupped to his belly, mewing. Its life so far has had none of the quality of life it should. He must do something for it before it has no life at all. He must give it knowledge of peace and pleasure.

He rises and dashes through the apartment, wondering how to hold off bombs, the armed men, their hatred.

He runs nude onto the balcony. Fireworks are exploding in the sky. Shot from somewhere just over the tall fence, their light is close enough to brighten him. People cheer and jabber. The sea reflects the light.

He hears that from above a coarse voice calling out: "A wedding! A wedding!
Don't be afraid!" The large head of the boy he saw in the entrance of the building this afternoon is leaning over the rim of the roof, waving with one hand and pointing to the fireworks with the other. "A wedding only!"

The phone rings him awake in the morning. He carries the kitten to the living room where he lifts the receiver. It is Ms. Malak. She says, "You sound better."

"Yes. I feel better." Indeed, his head is clearer than it was before, and though his ear still aches, it does so only slightly. He sets the kitten on the stone floor, where it seems to wake, opening up its paws and then yawning.

"What have you done to yourself?"

"I haven't done anything to myself." The kitten tries to stand but its legs tremble and it soon slumps down.
"I mean, what have you done *with* yourself since I saw you."

"I walked all around yesterday, trying to get my bearings."

"Bearings?" she whispers this in a way that he finds sinister. "There are no bearings here, Doctor. This is chaos."

"What?"

"Don't worry yourself too much, Doctor," she says, her voice normal now.

"What did you say about chaos?"

"I don't speak of chaos."

"What did you say?"

"You know the essential things you need to know." She sounds cheerful.

"I'm not sure that's true. I don't know anything about my job, for example."

"Are you drinking enough water? It is easy to get overly dry. Are you eating enough? Be careful with fruits. Wash them in bottled water, or use tablets of chlorine. This is what Dr. Sarkis told me I should tell you. There are certain things of which an outsider must be careful."

"All right. What I am trying to ask you—"

"Don't go out very much alone at night and certainly in no instance should you got to the south or the east of the city because these places are not secure."

He looks out the window. "Which direction is south?"

"From your apartment, the sea is to the south."

He realizes that if what she has said is true, he is on some type of peninsula. This seems unreasonable and he wonders if she is lying to him. The kitten raises its head and mews. Its eyes are gummed almost completely shut. It mews again.

He closes his own eyes.

"There was a man, an American, beheaded."

"Here?"

"Of course not, Doctor. It was in the place of your most recent troubles."

"My most recent troubles?"

"Not yours, Doctor. Your country's."

"Beheaded?"

"Yes. Certainly there will be others. Certainly other Americans will be taken and treated in such a way."

112

"That won't happen here?"

"Who is to say? In any case, Dr. Sarkis told me I should tell you these things. He said that I should tell you this carefully so as not to make you afraid. Are you afraid?"

Indeed, a feeling of fear has passed over him. He opens his eyes and looks at the kitten. He says, "I don't think so. It's more a matter of figuring out how I got here and what I am doing."

"Are you sure that you aren't afraid?"

"I just want to know what is going on."

"Of course, as I told him, you don't look very American, so I suppose this may keep you safe. Still, if they want to find Americans, they know where to look. There is a history of them finding Americans here." Her voice has gotten low again.

"You are playing a game with me."

"Excuse me?"

"Ms. Malak, won't you talk to me about the nature of my job or how I came to get it?"

"Doctor, you're a very direct person."

"I don't know if I am typically direct, but I feel a little desperate now."

"These questions are for Sarkis."

He lifts the kitten and puts it on his lap, saying, "Maybe then you can help me in another way. I found a cat, quite sick . . . ."

"The campus is covered with sick cats."

"This one was quite small and very sick."

"Really, Doctor. I hope you have not brought it into the apartment."

"I did."

"You should not have even touched it."

"But I did touch it. And it needs help."

"It may seem that everybody is in need of some kind of help. Do you intend to be a hero for them all, Doctor?"

"I'm not trying to be a hero."

"What are you trying to be?" He thinks for an answer but nothing appropriate comes to him. Ms. Malak says, "In any case, I must be going. I've told you what I was asked to tell you."

"Ms. Malak, why won't you tell me any—"

The phone clicks dead.

After cleaning the kitten's eyes and determining that it still does not recognize tuna and milk as nutrition, or perhaps that it does not recognize nutrition as necessary, he decides to give it a bath in the kitchen sink. It emerges with its fur flattened against the bones of its chest, which seem terribly thin and an impossible many. Panic begins to overtake him as he realizes the bath was bad for the kitten. It seems now closer to death than it did before. He imagines taking the kitten to the top of the stairs where he found it and leaving it there. He takes a deep breath. Then he begins to count backward from ten. By the time he reaches seven, everything is clear to him. He does not need to give up. He will call Manal, and she will help him do what he needs to do.

She answers, "'Allo?"

"Manal?"

"'Allo? Yes?"

"You met me yesterday, at the internet café."

"Yes, I know. It's nice that you call. You are okay?"

"I'm well, but I found this cat who is very sick. Is there a veterinarian?"

"Wait one moment and I'll call you back. What number?"

He looks at the white card on the dial pad of the phone, but it is blank. "I'm at the Institute, but I don't know what extension my apartment is."

"Okay. Wait."

He feels a long time has passed. He believes she has put the phone down and forgotten him, though he knows this is an unreasonable belief. Five or so minutes seem to pass during which he holds the wet kitten in his palm and feels the sense of hopelessness re-take him. Just as he is ready to accept that the line has been abandoned, Manal comes back on. She

114

reads him a phone number. The hopelessness dissipates. He believes in Manal and the number she has given him. He believes in himself and his ability to do what should be done.

"Would you like that I should come?" she asks.

"Very much. But I have to take him now. He's so wet and small, he looks next to death already."

"It's okay," she tells him. "The kitten will be okay."

"Thank you."

He calls the vet, who speaks a clipped English. He sounds angry or tired or both, and he says he is leaving in fifteen minutes on a call to the south of the city and will not wait beyond those fifteen minutes. Then he adds, more softly, "Please hurry."

He promises he will, and asks for the address.

"Have your driver call me on your cell along the way. I will explain to him."

"I haven't got a cell phone."

"Everybody in this country has a cell."

"I haven't."

Sounding weary again, the vet spells the address.

After hanging up, he feels daunted by the prospect of getting where he should as quickly as he should. Perhaps he should call Manal back and tell her he'll wait for her to come and accompany him to some other vet that they will take their time in choosing, but he feels overly anxious and the idea of sitting still with the kitten to wait for Manal is unbearable. He folds the bottom half of his shirt into a sort of hammock into which he puts the kitten. Throughout the elevator ride down and across the parking lot, the kitten remains motionless, but it keeps its eyes open. He is not certain, but he thinks he feels it purr.

"What do you have?" the guard at the sea gate wants to know.

"A cat, who is sick."

The guard shakes his head. "They are all sick."

There is another figure in the guard booth. After a moment, a tall, exceptionally well dressed man with a narrow waist and wide shoulders steps forth. He is carrying an unlit

115

cigarette. His hair is neatly cropped and combed to the side, and his thin moustache is well manicured. Though his eyes appear kind, his face is compact and hard-edged.

"Doctor, I'm Captain Shalack."

"Hello."

"You have with you a cat?"

"I . . . I'm taking it . . . I have no time." Afraid that if he pauses for even a moment more, one of the men will try to stop him, he steps around Captain Shalack and rushes out to the street. He then takes fifteen or so quick steps down the sidewalk. A taxi approaches, honks, and he waves it over.

The driver speaks to him in Arabic.

"English?"

"No."

"A little?"

"No."

"French?"

"No."

"I'm in such a hurry."

The driver begins speaking in Arabic with a young couple standing alongside the fence. The man says, "He wants to know if you want him to take you."

"Yes. To the vet on this paper. But very quickly. Tell him if he can't make it in fifteen minutes, we shouldn't go. It has to be in fifteen minutes."

The man and the driver exchange a few sentences, and then both look at the paper and discuss it. The kitten is trying to climb out of his shirt. The men seem to be speaking more slowly than necessary. The woman is peering at the kitten.

"He is sick?"

"Yes."

The woman nods.

The man says, "Okay, he'll take you. It will be twenty minutes."

"All right. *Yella.* Let's go." He realizes he's used an Arabic word only after he is sitting in the front seat of the moving cab. He wonders where and how he learned it. It doesn't matter. They are driving along the sea, toward the veterinarian, where the kitten will be made well and his own heart will be put at ease. He is glad to be in the hands of the driver who maneuvers his car with apparent confidence. The driver speaks to him in Arabic again, pointing to the kitten. He nods and smiles, and the driver smiles too, looking forward.

The kitten has curled up on itself. He strokes its head and thinks of the idea that there is true goodness in him, regardless of what he comes from and what he has done. That he has been witness to and maybe even participated in a recent tragedy comes to him with certainty but he shakes any knowledge of it out of his mind. "It doesn't matter," he tells the kitten. "You matter."

They pass a crumbling section of the city where the insides of buildings are blackened and the outsides ragged. Cats and dogs and people all thin and furtive can be seen beyond the glassless windows, moving through rooms with half walls and some with no walls at all. Then they are on a busy, tight street with people of darker skin selling fruits and nuts and plastic toys in front of shacks piece-melded together. Then they are on a wide, arcing street like a freeway which takes them in a half circle and then straightens toward what he thinks is the east. The glass between him and everything he sees outside of the cab seems very thick or like the glass of a television screen so that what happens on the other side doesn't mean much.

He looks at his watch. Twenty minutes have passed. The driver's face shows the same surety as it did before, as if he is unaware of the time.

"Are we close?"

The driver glances at him and at the kitten and speaks in Arabic. Then he looks forward. They exit the freeway and are now in another ramshackle neighborhood. The diver slows the car. At each intersection, he looks left and right with apparent confusion.

He realizes it is too late. The time has passed. The kitten sleeps, but they will not reach the vet. Black desperation comes over him. He tells himself to calm. He will return home, call Manal, ask her to take him and the kitten to a different vet.

117

It is morning yet. He panicked before and acted too quickly. He can do things properly now.

"Let's go back," he says to the driver. "The vet has already left and nobody is waiting for us."

The driver keeps driving.

"Let's go back," he says more loudly. "*Yella*," he tries.

The driver speaks in Arabic and keeps driving. He pulls suddenly to a stop before an electronics store and jumps out. He runs into the store and then immediately returns for the address. Inside again, the driver talks with the man for a few minutes. He comes back, saying, "Okay, okay," and he drives. Forty minutes have passed. The driver's face is sweaty, and he no longer smiles. The car turns again and again. The driver stops once more for directions.

He has given up on trying to get the driver to turn around. He is trying not to give up on the kitten all together. It seems to shiver. He rolls the shirt up around it. Though he has given up on this trip, he doesn't know how to stop it. He watches dully as they pass shops they seem to have passed before, vendors he perhaps recognizes. And yet the driver goes on more frantically than ever, sweat holding the tips of his hair together, focus in his eyes, fingers occasionally rising from and then curling back on the wheel.

Then they are there.

It is a small shop, and it is not closed.

The driver smiles proudly.

The veterinarian, a tall man with a well-trimmed beard and serious eyes, is waiting with his assistant, a young woman with hair dyed brightly red. She wears a crucifix on her dark throat. The vet takes the kitten and speaks quickly to the assistant, who affixes a reddish light on a steel post beside a steel examination table. The assistant holds the kitten while the vet pokes a thermometer into its anus. It squirms but does not squeal and does not otherwise fight.

"Thirty three degrees."

"What does that mean?"

"He is dying. It should be thirty eight." The vet sounds angry.

118

"What can you do?"

"Keep him warm. We will use a needle to put food into his body. We will do what we can."

The kitten tries to curl its front paws beneath its chest. The assistant keeps a single finger on its backbone.

"I should leave him with you?"

"Of course."

He reaches for his pocket and realizes he has only two bills there. "Are they big enough?"

"No, nothing. When he is well you can pay."

"Thank you, Doctor."

"It's nothing."

He stands staring at the kitten on the table in the red light. He thinks of the I.V. with which they will feed the kitten, the needle that will sink into its skin and be taped there. He thinks of the day and the night the kitten will spend alone. Perhaps, he thinks, it will be many days and nights with not much more than the warmth of the light. He thinks that the kitten should know—but of course cannot know—all of this pain and isolation is meant to help. He thinks that the only way any of this will be worth the suffering the kitten has begun to endure is if the kitten has a perfect life afterwards. He thinks that he will give it that perfect life.

"It's okay," the assistant says to him.

He realizes his eyes have grown wet. He feels very tired. The driver, who has been standing behind him the entire time, cups his shoulder. They walk out together and drive back slowly. He tells himself that he will do what he can. He will make himself stick here. He will buy the kitten toys. He will give the kitten love. He will protect the kitten. Everything he does will be for the kitten.

When they arrive at the sea gate to the Institute, he gives the driver the two bills. The man does not look at him but speaks in a low, flat voice.

"Is it not enough or is it too much?"

The driver glances at the bills and away from them.

"Listen, I'll go get more. You wait here. I promise I will come back. I'll go get more." He speaks like this until he believes the driver will believe he is saying something he should. The driver still has not taken the money from his hands and he lays it on the seat as he gets out.

Now the driver peers up at him with questioning eyes.

"I'll be right back," he says again.

He takes all the money he has left in his kitchen drawer and returns as quickly as he can. The taxi is gone. He thinks of the unpaid driver moving off slowly through the traffic and then walks slowly back past the guard—Captain Shalack was not there upon his return and is not there now—and toward his apartment, afraid of its emptiness, afraid of himself within that emptiness. He stops and looks all around.

He walks toward the stone steps leading to the neighborhood above, reminding himself of his resolve to build a life in which he will be able to offer something of value to the kitten.

He thinks now that the smell that pervades the streets is more than the oil and more than the food, but that it is all these elements and the pollution he can see hiding the coast to the north—or is it the east?—and something deeper. Something less tangible than any of those things. He has turned right from the upper Institute entrance this time, and soon he passes a movie theatre, in the lobby of which sit two men on beat up looking wooden chairs. One of the men appears to be about fifty and is tall with curly hair and a kind face, and the other man is perhaps fifteen years younger. The younger man has light green eyes and wears a Denver Broncos baseball cap and drinks from a plastic cup. Both of the men greet him with nods as he looks around the lobby. The posters all along the wall advertise American sexploitation films from the 1970's.

"Is this all you offer?"

"Not pornos," the curly haired man says emphatically, waving a single finger. "*La-ah.*"

"I understand."

"No pornos."

"I just wondered if you have any other movies."

"This is all we have. Even what you see in the posters is cut out," the curly-haired man says. "All the parts with bare asses."

"But a little makes it through," says the other man.

"A very little," says the curly haired man.

"Nothing like what you see in the States. That's where you from, isn't it?" the younger man says.

"Yes." He immediately likes the man for knowing this about him.

"I have a home in Texas, a wife and child there." He stands and offers a hand. "Ayman," he says. "I import."

He nods.

"And export."

He nods again.

"This is Alex," Ayman says.

Alex stands and, smiling, shakes hands as well. "Sit, sit with us."

There is a small plastic chair against the far wall, and he brings it over closer to the chairs of the two men. As he sits, a small, very dark man enters with apparent shyness. After circling around the walls as if studying the posters, he sidles up to Alex and hands him two blue bills, then goes up a set of stairs. He is passed by a short man coming down the steps. The short man does not leave the lobby but walks through a set of dark curtains. This theatre is soon exited by yet another man who looks up the stairs, then over at Alex, to whom he says something in Arabic. After Alex answers, the man nods and goes up. He is passed by another man going down; this man then disappears through the curtains. After a moment of calm, a completely different man descends, pauses before the lobby curtains, then parts and peers between them before letting them fall closed and goes back up the steps.

"They wander like that," Alex says, "from film to film, hoping to see the parts that have been cut out."

"And all they have to do," Ayman says, "is watch cable television after midnight. Everything in Beirut is allowed if you look in the right place. Small minds, that's the problem. I got ahead because I have a big mind, right Alex?"

Alex nods sincerely.

"You have to think with a big mind. If you want sex, you don't come slipping around a little theatre like this. You get the cable. You go to the brothels. And if you don't have money to go to the brothels, you get it. You find a way. If you can find a thousand for these crappy films, you can find thirty thousand for the brothels."

"Ayman, the brothels aren't good," Alex says.

"Ah. Anyway. I prefer though to spend my time in the Philippines. That is the size of my mind. For sex, I go to the Philippines."

Ayman lifts a half bottle of whiskey and pours a shot of it into a plastic cup. He motions with it to a bag of ice. "Do you want any?"

"No ice, thanks."

Ayman shrugs and hands him the whiskey.

Alex is drinking a beer in a can. He points to his stomach and squeezes his hands tightly. "I have pain here if I drink whiskey."

"Esophagus?" he asks.

Alex looks uncertain.

"Yes," Ayman says, "his esophagus. Or maybe it is an ulcer. Everybody in Lebanon has ulcers. Ever since the war."

"I thought it was called the incidents."

Ayman looks at him with surprise. "Only the assholes call it that. What are they going to call the next one?"

"The next one?"

"Yes. All the assholes are sitting around waiting for the next one. You think the lines are gone? Big lines and little lines. All the lines are all right here. If people thought they could afford it, they'd be fighting now. They'll be fighting again. And then when they pretend it is over they will have to think of something to call it. You now say your war is over, but it's just started."

Alex's face looks somber and he drinks from his beer. "Yes, Ayman, you're right. It is the business in Iraq. It stirs the people up."

"They were stirred up before. They've always been stirred up and always will be. It was only better hidden before the Americans went into Iraq."

An old man wearing a red and white checkered kerchief around his head enters, speaking slowly to the three of them. Ayman ignores him. Finally, Alex rises and takes two blue notes from his billfold and gives them to the man. Ayman shakes his head.

"Alex is stupid to give it to him. They are Syrians mostly, these beggars, or fakers. The women take out the children of three others and beg. Some of the men cut off their feet or hands. They mangle up their faces to get sympathy."

"Ayman," Alex says, "it's harder work than what we do, isn't it? They have their jobs."

Alex shrugs. "He calls it a job what they do. He thinks their job is to make him feel good about himself, don't you Alex?"

Alex nods. The man has started toward Ayman, talking softly in Arabic, but Ayman hardens his eyes and half rises as if he is ready to lunge at the man. The man says several words quickly and then turns, bows to Alex, and leaves the theatre.

Ayman eats a nut from a bowl on the floor. He takes a drink of his whiskey, then leans back in his chair. "You know," he says, "we get what we earn."

"That's a Western attitude," Alex says.

"That doesn't make it wrong. And some things that people call Western are not so Western. It is just our excuse for behaviors we don't admire in ourselves. I have a lover, a mistress in the Philippines. I'm not ashamed. I work like a dog, and buy my wife—she's an American—a big house, swimming pool, three thousand square feet—the house. She is always on me anyway. When I come home to her it is better if I've been to my woman in the Philippines first. " Ayman takes a quick drink, looks into the cup, and then takes another. He says, "I was just there. She says, 'Ayman, I miss you so much, when are you coming back?' For ten thousand dollars a year, I keep her in a very nice place with everything she needs. She works a little. Everywhere I go, I just like to have fun. That's what she likes about me. We were on a bus this last visit, and there were only just these Philippinoes and me. I was drinking whiskey. I said to one guy, 'Drink with me, I don't drink alone.' He says, 'No, no.' I say, 'Yeah, it will put hair on your chest.' 'Oh,' the man says, 'yes?' So soon we are all drinking from this bottle. I take underwear out of my bag and put it on my head. I have them all singing in English Old Macdonald. Eee iiii eeee iiii ohhhhh." Ayman laughs.

Alex laughs.

He laughs along with them. The whiskey goes down well. He is by now used to the dark figures coming in and out of the curtains, up and down the steps. He takes a nut from the bowl. It is overly salty and makes him want to drink again. He does. They all drink. They sit in silence for awhile, drinking and eating nuts. Alex waits on several customers. Ayman tells a story about a woman in Dubai—a Middle Eastern country of which he is vaguely aware—who was married to a British teacher and would meet Ayman afternoons to kiss behind a fountain. "I could never figure out how to fuck her." He shrugs and they fall to silence.

After a little while, a well dressed woman passes by and Ayman follows her with his eyes.

"You like Lebanese women?"

"They look good."

"Damn right."

"Once, only once, she—my lover, not my wife—let me bring another pussy into the bed. Now she is too jealous." He shrugs. "Alex, you ever have two pussies?"

Alex chuckles and shakes his head.

"Alex," Ayman says, "is from a very religious family. It is one thing to show these cut up movies but another thing to have pussies. His brother owns this place. But Alex comes here six days a week and works. You know how much he makes?"

"How much?"

"They pay Alex $300 a month, U.S. You understand? It is like that here. Everybody is poor or rich. There is no

124

middle class. Nobody marries. Everybody lives with his parents, who have established homes already. Alex lives with his mother and father who have money from before. He is forty seven years old and lives like that."

"It is true," Alex says. "I make enough to buy beer and lunch. I work for that. Everybody works like that."

He nods. A slight fear comes over him concerning his own financial status. He has used over half of the Lebanese money in the drawer. He wonders how much he is making and whether or not he'll be able to legitimately stay in this place with it.

"But you see, Ayman, by what you say, we should think about those unlucky ones who have to beg to eat."

"No, no. First, they are Syrian usually. They are not of this place and should not have come here. Second, even if they have to live on three hundred a month they should be doing it. Like the first war, the next war will be many wars. It will include a class war. Me, I got lucky, but I made my luck happen. And I won't stay here. I come to see my mom and dad, my brother. People either want to stay or go. I said, 'I will go into the world where things are better.' Now I travel, make my home in Texas, but I see the world. The Philippines." He smiles deeply.

"Ayman, Ayman." Alex says, shaking his head.

He wonders if Ayman is lying about his home and wife in Texas and about his mistress in the Philippines. He wonders if Alex knows Ayman is lying. He wonders if they sit here every day lying. He does not begrudge them these lies. He thinks, in fact, to invent his own stories with which to entertain and further connect with them.

Ayman's cell phone rings. He clicks it open.

"Hi, honey." He winks, and then speaks in a near falsetto. "Yes, I miss you too. I don't know when I'll get back, though. I know, but me too, honey. Does it rain there? What time do you have? Oh, yes. All right honey. I have to go. I love you, too."

He clicks the phone down grinning.

"She's never had enough of me. I wish I could pass through on my way back to the States."

"How long will you be gone this time?" Alex asks.

"A month, maybe more. As long as I can stand the woman. She's getting fat, sitting there in the big house I build for her. I should call her now. Shit, I can't. Let us get drunk and then I will. Let us get drunk. I will call her and tell her I love her and that I can't wait to get home and see her."

Ayman drinks the last of what is in his cup and then pours himself another one full to the top. "What time is it, Alex?"

"I don't know."

He finishes his drink and looks into the empty cup. Now that it is apparent Ayman has not been telling lies, it seems not such a good idea to invent stories about himself. The truths he does not want to tell, not even to himself. He says, "I have to go."

"What are you going to do?" Ayman asks.

"I should call this girl I met." It is the first excuse that comes to his mind, although he realizes, when he says it that he really does want to call Manal.

Ayman raises his eyebrows. "Tell her to bring her sister. Or a friend. We'll go out tonight, who knows, get lucky? Lebanese women are very aggressive in some ways. The one who wants to marry you, she is worthless. But the one who wants to enjoy you…" He turns to Alex. "You know how long it's been since I've had a Lebanese pussy?"

"How long?"

"Years. So have her bring a friend, a sister, something, anything."

"It's nothing like that. She just means to show me around."

Ayman rises and looks at him skeptically. "Call her, tell her to bring a sister or a friend. It's not best for you to be out alone anyway. Do you know what areas are secure? Do you know who to trust? I know. Here, take my phone and make the call." Ayman thrusts the cell phone forward.

He stares at the phone. Ayman juts it toward him aggressively.

"Okay." He accepts the phone and digs the number out of his pocket. Ayman's eyes have gone hard and he turns away from them to step into the street. He dials the number, hoping she will not answer because he does not want to talk to her while Ayman and Alex watch.

"'Allo?"

"Hi, Manal."

"Hi! How is the cat?"

"I think he's going to be okay."

"I came to where you live but you had left."

"How did you know where to go?"

"I know the Institute. But they told me at the gate you had gone."

"It's okay. I found my way. I'm sorry that you waited on me."

"You sound… what is the word? Sad?"

"Tired. It feels like it has been a long day."

"I don't work tonight. I could show you the Dunes center."

Ayman has risen and is walking toward him. He holds out his hand for the phone, saying, "Let me talk to her."

"Well, I'm sorry you can't," he says into the phone. "Maybe some other time."

He pushes the hang up button and shrugs to Ayman, who grimaces. An anger seems to overtake Ayman's face as he snatches the phone. "You couldn't convince her?"

"No."

"I could have convinced her."

"I imagine so."

Ayman stands looking at him.

"I suppose I ought to go."

"Go then." Ayman shrugs. They shake hands, and Ayman's eyes soften again. "Come back sometime"."

"Yes," Alex says, and embraces him slightly. "You are welcome here."

Walking through the Institute, he is overwhelmed by the sense that despite the fact he has found his way around, and that he has found a doctor for the kitten, something like friends to drink with, a woman who may show him around, he has no real idea of where he is. This realization is accompanied by an even more frightening sense that he still hasn't really figured out who he is and that perhaps he doesn't want to.

"Doctor?"

He turns and sees the well-dressed man he met at the lower campus earlier in the day. "Captain Shalack," he answers, surprising—but not necessarily pleasing—himself by remembering the man's name.

"I wanted to more fully introduce myself," Captain Shalack says gravely. "You went away so quickly."

"Yes. I'm sorry."

"Did you take care of your cat?"

"I took him to a veterinarian."

"It is rare to find a person here who cares." Captain Shalack says this in a way that suggests not compliment but mere observation. He adds, "I don't suppose it is easy to find people anywhere who are capable of showing care."

"I don't know."

They walk together toward the top of the steps that climb down the hill and toward his apartment.

"I've wanted to see that you have settled well."

"I'm working on it."

"You find your apartment comfortable?"

"Yes."

Captain Shalack nods. "The guards have treated you with respect?"

"Very much so."

Captain Shalack takes from his pocket a package of cigarettes which he regards for a moment before shaking one out. "Good. Our motto has to do with security and courtesy. I would repeat it to you, but you can imagine the idea of it. Can I offer you a cigarette?"

"No, thank you."

They have reached a shaded bench near the top of the steps, where Captain Shalack pauses to put the cigarette in his mouth. "So you have passed through our gates a few times already. That is, of course, normal. And it is quite safe, especially in terms of the immediate area. You know they are doing to other American civilians in other parts of the Middle East."

"Yes."

Captain Shalack puts his foot on the bench and leans his elbow on his knee, staring out toward the sea. "We are all watching out for you."

"Watching out for me?"

"Yes. We have your best interests in mind."

He continues on, reaching the top of steps before turning and saying, "Thank you."

Captain Shalack draws from his pocket a lighter and flicks its flame to the tip of the cigarette. After drawing of it and releasing the smoke, he says, "And of course, your apartment is yours. Regard it is you would your own property."

"Thank you."

"You may have guests. You may come and go as late as you like. People talk as if Beirut, and especially the Institute itself, is full of eyes. That may be true. Perhaps who visits who is always known." Captain Shalack pauses here and appears to peer at him meaningfully. "But we want you to feel as comfortable here as if you were at home. I personally want you to feel that comfort."

"Good night, Captain."

"Good night, Doctor."

He begins down the steps. The impression that he is followed causes him to stop near the bottom of the steps. Turning quickly to look behind him, he finds nothing but a few cats. Indeed, they watch him.

Then, by accident, he notices from where else he is watched. At the top of his building is the large head of the boy he yesterday spotted in the entrance to the building, the same boy who, late last night, shouted down that the explosions

129

where only of wedding celebration fireworks. The boy raises his hand in a wave.

He waves back.

And then the boy disappears quickly.

He understands that if he does not make it to his elevator before the boy makes it down, they will have some type of conversation. At this time, the idea does not appeal to him. He jogs quickly down the rest of the steps and starts across the large parking lot between the two buildings, but he isn't even at the entrance to his side of the building—it is divided into two parts—before the boy comes lumbering out the entrance at the opposite end.

He stops and watches the boy approach. The boy appears seventeen or eighteen and is gangly. "Can you come up?" The boy's accent is thick and his words are further slurred by what seems an unnatural deepness in the boy's voice. All his features are large, his nose, his teeth, his ears. He wears a Marine style crew cut.

"Sorry?"

"For a little time come?"

"What's your name?"

"Fadi," he says.

"You want me to come up now?"

"We will go from here," the boy says, pointing to the other side of the building.

Fadi stares at him expectantly. He doesn't want to go, but he senses that the boy will be persistent and that it will require more energy to dodge the invitation than to go with Fadi. He follows Fadi to the other side of the building and into the elevator there. Going up, he notes that scratched in the paint on the inside of the door are two messages he recognizes from his own elevator. *Mas Futbar* and *For I Have Seen The Fruits*. For a moment, he is convinced that he has become disoriented and that, indeed, this is his elevator, but then he settles into the fact that this is not his elevator and the words have simply been scratched into both of them.

From the landing on the eighth and final floor, a small set of stairs climb higher yet. Fadi smiles and leads the way up

130

them. He pounds the flat of his hand on the door and then opens it. They step into a small room, crowded with plants and framed photographs, mostly of babies. There is a tiny television and two couches as well as a stuffed chair, all fairly worn.

"Come," Fadi says.

They walk out through a narrow doorway and are standing on the roof, overlooking the campus and the sea. He steps carefully over a mess of electrical cords and follows Fadi around the side of the small edifice. In its shadow sits a plastic table with six plastic chairs around it, and, to his surprise, three women, two of whom are young, and sharply dressed, and pretty.

Fadi introduces him as "Doctor," and he thinks fleetingly about correcting the boy, but does not. He smiles at the three women, Mama, Nadine, and Dany. The girls wear long black hair and have narrow, dark eyes, prominent cheekbones, clear smiles. Nadine, the shorter, and, he thinks, younger of the two, keeps her head turned to the side. Dany stares at him. The mother greets him warmly with her hands and smile. She says a series of words that might be English but are undecipherable to him. He nods and smiles. As he is about to sit, he notices a mesh crib pressed against the side of the little building. It contains two very fat, dark babies, each swaddled in several layers of clothing.

He leans forward to look at them. One of them sleeps and the other sits up, smiling at him, streams of sweat running from its hair down the bridge of its nose.

"Which of you do they belong to?" he asks the girls.

"*Shu?*" Nadine says, covering a smile with the back of her hand.

"*La-ah!* Mama watches them. We help," Dany says. "We watch them until their mothers come from work."

"Right. I'm sorry." The mother disappears around the corner. He sits. The air moves freely up here, and he cannot smell the city or the sea.

"He's American," Fadi says.

"*Shu*, Fadi," Nadine says. "We know."

"He likes Americans," Dany says.

Nadine dips her head to the side again. Her face is of delicate bone structure and her neck is very thin. He can see the rounded ends of her collarbones standing out.

Dany says, "It has been a long time since we've had Americans. Sometimes they come to teach for a little while, but since the war they have not been much here." Her eyes are hooded, her nose long and slender, her chin strong.

"The war in Iraq?"

"Our war."

"Oh, the incidents."

Fadi gives a nervous laugh.

"Do I look like an American to you?"

Dany shrugs.

Nadine smiles, covering it again, and tipping her head further to the side.

"Yes, yes, Americans," Fadi says.

"Do I look like one to you?"

"I know this," Fadi says.

The mother appears with a tray covered in fruit, the skins of which glisten. He wonders if they are safe and if the water they have been washed in is safe.

"*Kol*," she tells him. "*Kol*."

"Eat," Fadi says.

He means to say, "No thank you," but he can see expectation in the mother's face. He studies the tray: grapes; apples cut into fourths; strawberries; very small bananas, already peeled; white, glistening kernels he doesn't recognize. Finally, he takes a grape and eats it. The mother nods and disappears back into the building.

"*Sahtein*," Nadine says. She rises to look in at the babies. Through her thin blue shirt he can see her spine. She lifts out the baby that is sitting up and takes it back to the chair with her. It smiles widely.

"Have you met many people?" Dany asks.

"No, not really. Ms. Malak. Do you know her?"

Fadi shrugs and says, "*Yaani*."

"*Yaani*?"

"It means 'some'," Dany tells him.

"I just met Captain Shalack."

Fadi's mouth closes completely and he looks away. Nadine and Dany glance at each other and then down. The baby continues to smile.

"Did I say something wrong?"

The sisters exchange looks again. Fadi lets out an uncomfortable giggle.

Dany asks, "Do you like it here?" He notices that there is something elegant in the way she holds her back and moves her hands, as if she is moving from one pose to another, though he knows she is not doing this on purpose.

"Yes, I think so," he says. A breeze stirs her hair. Nadine lowers the baby. It takes several wobbly steps toward Fadi, who pats its head.

"I think I like it," he says.

Fadi begins to clumsily try to lift the baby. The baby pushes out of Fadi's grip and lumbers back to Nadine.

"Yes, I *do* like it." It's true. He feels more pleasant that he has felt since arriving—more pleasant than he can remember having ever felt—looking from sister to sister and then to the brother.

Nadine giggles.

"*Shu?*" Dany says. She smiles herself but does not giggle.

Fadi leans back, surveying the fruit with apparent pride. He plucks a piece of apple from the tray and plays with it for several moments before it slips from his fingers. He scoops it from the roof and then begins eating it.

"He is always like this," Dany says. "Playing."

The mother reappears with a pot and several cups. She puts one cup before each of them and then pours tea from the pot.

"Eat, eat," she says. "Drink *kaman*."

He picks up a strawberry and puts it in his mouth.

"*Sahtein*," the mother says. "And this," she says, pointing to the bowl.

"You call it quince, I think," Dany tells him.

He spoons a few kernels into his mouth. They explode against his teeth and the juice inside of them reminds him that he is thirsty. All the fruit looks to him now like water contained in skins.

The mother dashes off again.

Nadine says something he can't hear.

"What?"

"She says you make work as a teacher here?"

"Yes, I think that's it. Yes, definitely."

"Are you afraid?" asks Dany.

"Of what?"

"All the Americans to come after were afraid. From here we saw a man taken once, into a car. He was a teacher. He tried to fight them and they beat him. His blood was on the entrance on your side of the building for many days. Then it got worn away. His glasses were there for longer than that. One of the sides was broken. I think nobody wanted to pick them up."

"All that trouble is over, isn't it?"

Fadi looks away and Nadine seems to follow his gaze.

Dany says, "*Yimkin*. Maybe. There is calm. But now there is Iraq. There are some here who don't want the peace. There are some people here who will find ways to make us divide." She shrugs. Her face has gone sad. He has the urge to reach toward it. She smiles at him and the sadness almost disappears.

Fadi lets out a gruff laugh. He picks up a strawberry. His fingers are huge, though his arms and neck are incredibly thin.

"They will fight again," Fadi says.

"*Shu?*" Dany demands. She and Fadi speak passionately in Arabic, and then Fadi rolls his shoulders and puts up his hands as if to silence his sister. She glares at him.

"Don't be afraid," Fadi says. "If they fight again, they fight."

"*La*, Fadi. No more talk like this," Nadine says.

"You are welcome here," says Dany. She smiles.

"Thank you. You all make me feel welcome."

134

"It was only a little blood. The bad part was the glasses," Fadi says.

"What happened to him—the teacher, I mean?"

Nadine looks to Dany, and Dany looks to Fadi, and Fadi looks to Nadine. "*Ma barif.* I don't know," Dany says. "That was a long time ago. We have known many good Americans and have had much fun with them," Dany says.

"This is true," Fadi says.

Nadine lifts the baby so that its head blocks his vision of her face. When she lowers the baby, he studies her mouth. He wants her to speak so that he can see her lips moving and her teeth behind them. He imagines kissing her.

"What do you do?" he asks.

Nadine looks away. Dany answers, "We help our mother. And we wait."

"What do you wait for?"

Dany shrugs. "Something different."

The mother reappears and pours more tea. She looks at the baby in the playpen, nods her head, and then sits. She smiles broadly at him. They are all watching him. He takes several grapes and another strawberry. He spoons more of the kernels into his mouth. He drinks his tea. The chair is comfortable and he realizes he is tired. He can imagine sleeping on the roof, letting the sky grow dark, feeling the wind come, watching the stars grow visible and bright. Twilight is not far off. Though he feels a sense of comfort, he feels too that it is time for him to go.

"I must leave now. I want to thank you."

Dany's eyes drop. Fadi looks with apparent concern at his mother. Nadine appears unchanged. The mother smiles at him. "You must go?"

"You've been very kind. I would like to come again. Can I?"

"Of course," Dany says. "We want you to."

"Yes, again," says Fadi. "*Kaman.*"

The mother nods.

Nadine stands, balancing the baby against his shoulder, and is the first to shake his hand goodbye. He can't remember after he has released it how it felt, and it is the same with Dany. Fadi walks him to the other side of the roof. There is another small building identical on the outside to the one in which they seem to make their home. In this one is a washing machine and a freezer, as well a small bed. A curtain cuts the room in half and he wonders if a bathroom of some kind is on the other side. Fadi takes several combination and key locks of off latches attached haphazardly on a scarred door, which he then opens. He points down a set of steps. "Your elevator is there," Fadi says.

"Okay. Thank you. Good bye"

He walks down the stairs instead of taking the elevator. The stairwell is surprisingly cool.

"This was a good day," he says. Though he has spoken quietly, his voice echoes amongst the stone walls. When he reaches the sixth floor, he sees that Manal leans against the wall in front of the door to his apartment. She has not yet seen him, and he stops for a moment to look at her. Her lips are pursed so that she looks pouty, or perhaps perplexed.

"Hi, Manal."

She turns quickly and her face makes as if to smile but then it does not. "I'm sorry I came without—"

"I'm glad you did."

"What you said on the phone was strange and I thought maybe you had trouble."

"Is it okay for you to come here alone?"

"My father brought me."

"Your father?"

"Yes, of course. I told him to see a friend that lives close. He trusts me."

"You had no trouble coming past the guards?"

"No."

"Did you see a man, well dressed, Captain Shalack?"

She drops her eyes. "No, not Shalack."

"You know of him, though?"

"He is a man well-known from the war. *Ma barif.*"

"You don't know?"

136

She smiles. "You're learning Arabic. I don't know. *Ma barif.*

"I guess I'm picking a few things up."

They stand not looking at each other for a few moments. He is aware of his hunger for her. It is an extension of the desire he felt for Dany and Nadine above, and it is a renewal of the desire he felt for Manal herself and the brothel girls yesterday. Again, he wonders if lust is one of his salient qualities.

"You have water." She points out a piece of paper taped to the elevator. He walks back to read it: "Despite the severe dryness of the season, we have somehow managed to save a bit of water in our reserve. We will now turn the water on for the full day, but we ask that you be mindful of your use of it, which we shall monitor closely. We hope we will not be forced by over-consumption to turn the water off again. Kindest regards, The Physical Plant."

"That's good news," he says. "Do you want to come in?"

"Yes."

"I think Ms. Malak left me tea. Maybe I can give you a cup," he says, using his key to unlock the door and then pushing it open.

"Okay." She steps through the doorway and stops immediately. She leans forward and peers around.

"Listen, I'll be back in just a second. Excuse me, okay?"

"Okay."

"You can come in more—all the way—if you like."

When he starts down the hallway, she is still standing just inside the doorway. He pees and washes his hands, which are shaking slightly with anticipation. He thinks as he dries them that he should be careful of what he gets himself, and her, into. He returns to the living room to find Manal sitting. She has turned on a light above the chair. She looks exceptionally small. He is aware of the narrowness of her waist and throat and wrists. Only her bosom—the cliché of a perfect bosom—is heavy. Without it, she would be so slight as to be insubstantial.

"Do you want tea?"

"Never mind. I don't feel like drinking tea." She smiles, but it is with uncertainty. She does not look at him and he studies her. He sees, as he stares, that the black hair above her ear descends far onto her face, like a sideburn. He sees, in fact, that she has something like a scant beard, downy but dark.

"You watch me," she says.

"You're beautiful," he says. It is true and not true, but he says it not in the name of truth but out of what he believes is near instinct. For the first time he can pinpoint since waking up, he is comfortable with this idea of his bodily hunger. That idea that what might be about to happen has happened before and will happen again, to nearly every living thing, that this desire for coupling is ancient, soothes him. He tells himself that there is no individual standard to which he should be held; he tells himself he is part of the mass throb of humanity, and that humanity is part of the mass throb of the animal world, and that lust is as basic a need as hunger and fatigue. He tells himself that the girl who sits across from his is not Manal, but a generalized girl, a representative female creature.

She turns her head in mock modesty and the hair on her chin stands out. Her midriff—exposed as thin and muscled beneath a three-quarters shirt—is marked by a downy line of hair as well. He supposes her nipples sprout hair, and that the area around her vagina must be more hairy than any vagina he has seen or imagined. In the hair of her head, pulled back with only a few curls dangling to the front, are white flakes of scalp.

He wishes he hadn't noted any of these things, but he knows that none of them will stop him. If he were sitting ten feet away, she would be only her figure, only the bone of her face, the cut of her eyes, with the hair of her cheeks and chin and the flakes of her scalp invisible.

She glances at him. Her eyes are so dark it is hard to tell the cornea from the pupil. Her teeth shine. She strikes him as both grotesque and angelic, and, in either case, untouchable, and yet he knows he will touch her. And he is certain of how she will react. As he stands to approach her, he feels something overwhelmingly hot burst in his belly, and he believes for a moment in spontaneous combustion. The heat dies down so there is only a slight and easy enough to ignore burning in his guts.

He reaches her.

The apartment has grown completely dark. When? How? He knows this place, but he can't place himself in it. He is leaning against his front door. The left side of his head hurts and that ear absolutely throbs. He feels a burn throughout his torso and a cramp in his belly. There is the sound of a toilet flushing. Manal comes from the hallway. He tells himself he is surprised to see her there, but he is not genuinely surprised.

"Okay," she says.

He cannot read her face. If he had a mirror, he thinks, he could not read his own.

They go out the front door and down the hallway and get into the elevator, where the light is dim and he can't see very well the hair that covers the whole of her. It is almost impossible now to believe in that hair, or if he can believe in it, he cannot believe he is repulsed by it. In fact, he can hardly believe in her, though she stands before him. She is beautiful. That they've just made love he is certain. He looks at her breasts, her abdomen, her curving thigh. He has freed her breasts from her bra, has taken off her panties. He has bitten and kissed and licked her. He has laid against her, pushed himself inside of her, held the small of her back and the curves of her ass in his hands.

And yet he can't remember it to prove it, nor can he tell how he really feels about it, or her, or himself in this situation.

The pictures he summons are of other girls, and they don't have names he can easily clutch, though they do have names. They are old pictures. He wonders where the new pictures are.

His shoulder itches. He remembers that while he was inside of her, there was a mosquito, the first familiar thing he saw after waking for the first time. He tried, he remembers now, to keep himself conscious of a desire not to kill the mosquito, but he can't remember if he maintained that consciousness through all the fucking or not. And the fucking itself is still only speculation.

The elevator stops and they walk through the lobby and out into the front parking lot. Two cars are parked there. He looks at them, wondering about their owners.

"I'll go by myself only to the gate. My father will be waiting. Of course, now I will tell him I've been alone with you, and we will get married."

"What?"

"*Ana am bemza.* I'm teasing."

Before his mouth touches hers, he can smell the scent of the city coming from it. Or maybe, he thinks, it is the scent of her coming out into the city. Now he can remember leaning into her and being aware of and slightly repelled by the smell. He can remember kissing her with a closed mouth and moving his mouth away from hers and the smell that came through it. He remembers putting his lips to the flesh of her neck and finding the taste of the smell there. She steps away, and he loses all sense of certainty about any of these memories.

"Not here. They watch us," she says.

She is a girl he has touched but he has no evidence. He can't imagine undressing her. Indeed, as she walks away, he longs for the fruit of her body as if it is a fruit he has never tasted. He longs to hold her. To be kissed by her and to be enveloped in her smell, whatever it is.

As he rides up alone in the elevator, he remembers previous lovers. Names come to him now, and faces come with them; he sees glimpses of moments from lovemaking and from seduction. He wants to give them—the women, the moments—meaning, but he cannot. They are simply images.

Inside the apartment, it occurs to him to call the vet; there is no answer. Perhaps the kitten sleeps in the light of the lamp. Perhaps he is comfortable, on his way to well, dreaming warm dreams.

The apartment building across from his is dark save a single light in a single window. He sees a figure move across it. He waits for several moments, wondering if he will see the figure again, but he does not.

On top of the bed sheets, he curls himself against a deepening ache in his gut.

He wakes dizzy and warm, with the feeling that something heavy has affixed itself with pincers to his stomach. Sitting up against the pain of its grip, he understands what is happening. At best, he has twenty seconds. He swings his feet to the floor and stands quickly. The sheet clings to his legs and hips as he stumbles through the doorway. Which way to go? Without time to reason, he turns left and realizes, after several steps, he has made the right choice. He stumbles through the bathroom door, twisting free of the sheet as he does, and then he skitters nude except for his socks across the floor. The toilet, tall and thin, stands with its lid open. He reaches it just as he feels his stomach begin to explode. With remarkable agility, he lands his ass against the seat; his head and neck push forward. Muscles all across his body tighten beyond any point he believes he has felt them tighten before.

It is all water, going on and on. It is, in fact, an incredible amount of water. More water than he can imagine in the human body, more water than he can imagine the toilet holding. He is aware of salt-like grains spitting out. The sea itself is gushing from him. The flow goes on and on. Suddenly, he is done. There are no final drops, no final spurts, nothing. He leans further forward, panting. Eventually, he turns to look into the toilet, but closes his eyes at the last moment and flushes. The smell that rises is the smell of the city and the girl.

His stomach feels crushed. In the mirror, it looks withered.

Despite the threatening notice he read on the elevator, he fills the entire tub with warm water and lies in it until it cools, and then he lets out some of the tepid water so he can add more hot. Through the rest of the night, he twists beneath his single sheet, trying to find a position that does not tighten any further the knot of his guts.

In the morning, he sits again on the toilet, trying to let himself uncoil, believing that with a final flow the sickness inside will be expelled and flushed. There is more substance to what he shits now, something grainy like seeds that burn. His stomach itself seems to run out of him and yet, after he has finished, he knows he has not gotten rid of what he must. His asshole is tender so that he does not want to wipe it. Tender too are the muscles of his stomach. He sits on the toilet feeling torn. Finally, carefully, he takes the last five or six sheets of toilet paper and uses them. Again, he does not face the mess in the toilet.

After a shower, he dresses. His stomach is tight but unmoving. He tells himself the worst is behind him and he can begin to do the things that must be done. Toilet paper, for one thing, is needed. Also, he must seek out the man to whom Ms Malak continually refers—Dr. Sarkis—and through him get an understanding of what his duties are and how he should prepare to perform them.

The elevator stinks of something that is like car exhaust, though he knows there are very few cars in the lot. When the doors open, he sees the foyer is covered with dark shuddering shapes. These are large roaches, on their backs, trying to turn. There are so many it is nearly impossible for him to walk through their jerking bodies without stepping on them. He wonders why they have come out from where they are hidden and what they are now doing. He recognizes that they are in some sort of distress, but he does not want to consider it overly long, nor does he want to give in to the desire to turn one or two of them over, for then, he knows, he will feel he must turn them all.

Outside, a rain falls. In fact, the weather has changed completely. The wind blows. The sky is gray. His guts harden as he crosses the lot and then they grow tighter with each step he climbs on the staircase that connects the lower-campus to the upper. A quarter of the way up, he begins to feel that any sudden movement could wiggle something loose from him.

It is more humid than he remembers it being the day before. His shirt is soaked through and when he touches his hair, his hand comes away damp. Halfway up, he stops and leans on his thighs, panting. He looks back down the steps and considers returning to his apartment. It is now apparent to him that he will soon have to shit again. "Toilet paper," he says out loud. "T.P." He tries to think of a joke to make about it to bring a smile to his face and ease his journey, but he has no such joke.

Most of the doors on the upstairs buildings are locked. Eventually, he discovers one that is open. Inside, the hallways are narrow. Their linoleum and walls are dirty. He searches for a restroom. All the doors are brown and some are marked by numbers pounded out of metal. Finally, he finds a restroom, but inside, there is neither toilet paper, nor any paper towels. He searches the hallways again until he finds a bulletin board with announcements on it. On one is Arabic lettering which surrounds a drawing of a traditional executioner holding an axe, as well as several figures in silhouette behind bars. Looking both ways before doing so, he tears the paper off. Beside it are two photocopies, each announcing a need for a teacher of English at elementary schools. He takes these as well.

His guts groan.

He walks gingerly back out into the gray. The rain has died down. He appraises the green slope of the hill down which the stone steps descend and the stretch of the sea steel blue below. He enjoys the view only until he thinks about the precision with which he must walk. Tiny step by tiny step, he finally reaches the bottom. There are several cars in the rear parking lot. Almost shuffling now, he makes his way toward the building.

In the foyer, all the roaches are still. It is obvious that they have been poisoned. They were dying before, and why he couldn't see that, or did not want to, he doesn't know. He walks just as cautiously as he did before so as not to step on any of them. The elevator jerks on the way up, and he worries that he might have let something pass into his underwear. Finally, there is the hallway, the doorway, his living room, the hallways to the bathroom, and the bathroom's open door.

Though the sky is cloudy, the bathroom seems full of light. Opening his ass, though painful, is also deliriously relieving. Then the ache in the guts subsides and the fire in his asshole numbs. He loses himself in this shitting and doesn't realize when he is done. It is only when his right arm experiences a sharp sensation that he comes to. A mosquito swollen with blood lifts away.

He rises, feeling light of head. This time he keeps his eyes open as he turns and looks down into a swirl of shit and blood he does not immediately identify as being shit or blood. Rather, it at first has the appearance of strange art to him, and he is transfixed. Then he remembers what it is and jerks his head up, closing his eyes as he does so. It seems unreasonable that something so ugly and of such a bad smell came out of him. He wipes with strips of the paper he took from the building above. So much of the mess clings to the porcelain even after he has flushed several times that he unhooks the shower nozzle and sprays the inside of the toilet bowl until finally it is clean.

Throughout the rest of the day, he adapts to a schedule: he shits; afterwards, for twenty minutes, there is a general sense of ease; then discomfort begins to build; after forty minutes of building, it reaches an almost unbearable point through which he must suffer for around ten minutes; then he shits, and the ease comes again.

He makes use of the time that immediately follows the shitting, when he is in the least amount of pain. He calls the vet but a man speaking only Arabic answers. He prepares tea though he doesn't drink it. He makes his bed. He looks through his things and makes a short list of what he must buy, food and cleaning materials. He takes a brief nap. The clouds diminish. The sky darkens with dusk. He notes that four windows across the way are lit. A few more cars are in the parking lot. He can hear voices below and see figures moving occasionally. Several cats are crying out. His stomach is bubbling.

His doorbell rings, but he does not answer it—the house stinks, perhaps he himself stinks. It is the shit; the poison; the smell of the girl; of the city; of the food; of everything. By now, he is exhausted. He shits a final time—forcing this one ahead of schedule—and then goes to bed. He is quickly asleep.

In the early morning, he dreams that he is moving swiftly toward Manal's chest. His face buries itself in her cleavage and then he uses his teeth so that her flesh tears and blood pumps out. She collapses away from him. He stands above her in semi-dark, a squirming kitten in each of his hands. He brings the first to his mouth and bites into its belly; he does the same with the second. He drops their torn bodies on the floor where they kick and try to rise. Then he bends to scoop up several giant roaches from the dozens scattered about. These he shovels into his mouth.

He chews.

Manal screams. The kittens scream. The roaches scream. His dream is all screams now; even he is screaming. He wakes, aware of the echo of at least his own scream in the apartment. Before he descends into sleep again, he tells himself that he would never hurt the girl or these animals. He tells himself that what he has seen is not a reflection of his own nature.

The phone rings him awake in the morning. Thinking it is the vet with news of the kitten, he leaps from bed and rushes down the hallway, his socks sliding him past the phone, for which he grabs, so that he sits down hard while at the same time pulling the receiver to his ear.

"Ugh," he says.

"'Allo?"

"Hello."

"It's me, Manal."

"Good morning, Manal."

He sits still, taking note of himself. The ache in his guts has slackened sometime during his sleep, but he is aware that he will need to shit within the next twenty minutes. There is a dull throb in his ear.

"I woke you?"

"It's okay." He sees that the sky and the sea are gray.

"I called only to say hi." She sounds nervous, or perhaps excited. "I want to—"

"Hold on," he blurts. He has nothing to say. He only knows that he doesn't want her to speak. She will try to arrange some kind of meeting, or she will engage him in a conversation meant to open another one, and, through it, some string of them by which he and she will grow close. It occurs to him that he doesn't want to see her again and thus never will. This causes in him a sorrow on her behalf. He says her name twice.

"Yes?"

"Thank you."

"Thank you?"

"I'm sorry."

"Why are you sorry?"

He is ready to tell her, but then he is uncertain of his recent conviction concerning the idea that he must avoid further contact with her. "I could be wrong," he says out loud.

"I don't understand," she says.

"About what I was thinking about myself."

"I don't know."

"*Ma barif,*" he says.

"Yes, like that."

The idea he's just had about never seeing her again frightens him now. He wants instead to tell her to come to him immediately. He wants to ask her to help him find himself and to help him, if what he finds is bad, to destroy that badness.

"You will be speaking like me in little time," she says.

146

At first, he thinks she means that his English will deteriorate, but then he realizes that, of course, she means his Arabic will improve.

He recognizes that both visions he has had regarding his future relations with Manal are too extreme. He imagines some practical middle ground in which they sit for tea at some café and talk, in which he neither pushes her completely out of his sight nor tries to bring her completely next to him.

"To stay here I'll want to know Arabic."

"We will practice. You will help my English and I will help your Arabic."

"Yes."

"I found all of you very nice," she says.

He wants to ask her to tell him what particular things about his mind and about his face she found nice. He believes that if he knew the answers to these questions about why she has chosen him for whatever it was he seems to be chosen, he would know everything he needs to.

"You too. I found you nice, too," he says. "But I must go now. There's a lot I have to do today."

"Okay. Goodbye."

"Goodbye."

After shitting and showering, he puts on a T-shirt, a dress shirt, and a tie. He studies his ass in his gray slacks. Nobody can tell from the outside, he thinks, how busy and how messy it has been.

The roaches are gone. Two men in dress jackets are walking across the parking lot, talking loudly in Arabic. He sees a child overly bundled for the heat trying to catch a cat. It dashes a few steps from the child's reach, stops, dashes away again, and then disappears into the green of the hillside. The child's mother, a pretty and plump woman, sits on a bench. He smiles first to the child and then to the mother, though neither responds, and he goes on. At the top of the stairs, he finds people milling about. All the buildings have their doors opened wide. He nods his head in approval.

He walks into the center of a grassy oval and looks to each of the three buildings around it, wondering which is home to his office and where he can find Dr. Sarkis.

Then he hears a voice he recognizes coming from the second floor of the building in front of him: Ms. Malak.

Inside, he climbs the stairs. She stands at her door, smiling stiffly. "Ah, Doctor. How nice to see you. You've only just missed Dr. Sarkis."

"I'm sorry for that."

"He'll be back perhaps later."

"You said I had an office. I wonder if I might see it. And my contract."

"Oh. Yes. We are standing in front of your office."

He follows the jerk of her head to a brown door with peeling paint. For decoration it has a red ribbon—the kind he associates with Christmas—taped to it. He tries the handle but finds it locked.

"If Dr. Sarkis had been here, he could open that door. But I cannot. In any case, I think they intend to renovate your office this morning."

He nods and leans toward the door, listening, though he can't imagine for what. He sniffs. The only smell here is of Ms. Malak's perfume, which is heavy.

He straightens. "What about the contract?"

"Yes. I'm sure you should like to see that. It will be arranged."

"Can't you show it to me now?"

She juts her chin forward and makes a clicking noise with her tongue. "I'm sure that if I could, Doctor, I would have told you."

His stomach rumbles, not painfully, but for several seconds, and fairly loudly. She takes what appears an unconscious step backward and looks away. He wonders if he should be seeking a toilet.

"If you are hungry," she says, "I recommend the Hard Rock Café. It is American, you know."

"Actually, I think they started in London."

She laughs as if he meant this as a joke.

"When do you expect Dr. Sarkis to return?"

"Perhaps after lunch."

"Where is the Hard Rock Café?"

She tells him to follow a path to a gate on the far end of the campus. From that gate, he should catch a *service*—a cab—going east. It is ten or so blocks in that direction. He doesn't tell her he can't figure out which way is east. Instead, he says, "Thank you."

It is fifteen blocks, and he walks it without minding. The gray cloud cover is moving out to sea and the color of blue it reveals is light and, he thinks, lovely. He pauses at the entrances to little shops, looking through the doors at the wares, trying to determine what places will be important for him to remember. The sidewalk is busy and grows busier. He tries a few times to greet people as they pass, but most respond with looks that suggest offense. Soon, he decides speaking or gesturing in such a way to strangers is not appropriate to the culture, and so he does not do it anymore. It is the first adjustment he is conscious of having made, and this pleases him as he continues down the narrow sidewalk.

He can hear eighties music—the music of his youth—coming out of the Hard Rock from twenty steps away. Inside, the music is so loud he realizes he would have trouble having a conversation in it. The café is empty, except for four members of its staff. With all of them watching him, he walks the circumference of the room, looking at the memorabilia hanging behind glass all along the walls: guitars, jackets, photographs with the famous signatures of famous musicians.

Though he is certain now of his hunger, he is somehow afraid to eat alone in this restaurant, beneath the gaze of the staff, the weight of all this memorabilia, and the sound of the music.

On the street again, he realizes his appetite is particular anyway. The thought of anything oiled doesn't appeal to him; neither does the thought of fruits or vegetables. Both these things, in fact, repulse him. What he wants, he realizes, is very specific: a coconut. What he settles for is a bag of mixed nuts

149

from a shop on the corner. Eating them as he goes, he makes his way back toward the Institute.

       .

    "Is my office ready?"

    Ms. Malak sits behind her desk, looking with a startled expression at him. "Ready?"

    "You said this morning they were renovating it. Have they started? Have they finished?"

    "Of course not so quickly." She glances from his face to the space beside it as if she expects somebody in the hall. He turns quickly. The hallway is empty. "Dr. Sarkis could have shown you your office," she says, "but you have missed him again. He is a very busy man. He left perhaps twenty minutes ago."

    "And my contract? You told me I could see my contract."

    "Yes, but again, you must see Sha—Dr. Sarkis. And he is not here."

    "When will he be back?"

    "I don't know. Perhaps I did not explain my position here. I'm not his secretary. I'm merely an instructor, and, during these summer months, the new faculty coordinator. That does not mean, however, that I keep his schedule or make his appointments."

    "But as the new faculty coordinator, don't you think you should be able to show me my contract? I don't feel very settled yet. There are things I need to know. Can't you get it for me and go over it with me? I want to feel settled. I'm working hard for that. I'm getting closer. Don't you want to help me?"

    "Really, Doctor, I've told you I can't. You've been here only three days. You're rather impatient, aren't you?" She rises and leans forward with her knuckles on the desk. "Perhaps you are not aware of how things are done in Lebanon. It's not uncommon for somebody to come from the West and insist on things being as they would in the West. But in fact, you are in Beirut. Here you are. There is nothing more you need immediately than I've given you."

150

Something not all together surprising nor at first overly daunting occurs to him. It is that there is no Dr. Sarkis.

"Okay, Ms. Malak," he says quietly. "I'm doing my best to make a go of it, but you're making it very hard. You keep telling me that here I am and that I should make the best of that. But you do not help me to make the best. "

"On the contrary."

"I give up on you." He pulls closed her door. He wonders, staring at it, why, if there is no Dr. Sarkis, she pretends there is one. A general sense of panic overtakes him. The panic gives way to a fear. The fear gives way to an anger, the power of which astonishes him. He can imagine himself kicking open the door to her office. He can imagine screaming questions at her. He can imagine picking things off her desk and throwing them through her windows. He can imagine then kicking open the door to his own office. Perhaps, he thinks, anger—even rage—is one of his defining qualities. If there was a side to him that he decided to escape, perhaps it was this.

He knocks on Ms. Malak's door and then opens it. He is not certain what he will do then.

"I'm sorry, Ms. Malak. I just really have many questions."

She stiffens her back. "I thought you had given up on me."

"I have now ungiven up on you."

"Your questions will be answered. But not right now, and not by me. May I tell you something, Doctor? You look a mess. Perhaps you are still ill. You need a haircut and a shave. You need to press your shirt. You need to put yourself in order before you meet Dr. Sarkis. There is still time."

"A haircut?"

"Yes."

"I don't look well?"

"Not at all. Your eyes are red. Your skin is white. You look ill."

"I've had stomach troubles."

"Of course, the running stomach."

"And the fever I arrived with."

"Yes."

"And some ache in my ear."

"You did not want to appear to be at the mercy of your sickness when you meet Sarkis."

"Dr. Sarkis?"

"Yes."

"What is his name?"

"Dr. Sarkis."

Her face seems to twitch when she says the name. He is right. There is no Sarkis. Perhaps Ms. Malak herself is in control. Or perhaps there is someone else who wants to remain anonymous. Perhaps it is Captain Shalack who is in charge. He realizes that aside from the family on the roof, the only people he has actually met on campus are Malak and Shalack. But for whatever reason, they mean to keep him in the dark. They mean to make sure he doesn't know what he is in for.

"I hope you haven't got me mixed up with somebody," he says.

"What do you mean?"

"I hope you all don't think there is something I have to give that you need. As far as I know, I haven't anything anybody would find of real value."

"We want your English, Doctor, and your name. An American name."

"Right. Okay. Thank you."

Down the hall from her office is a bathroom. In its mirror, he sees that he looks almost as bad as she said he did. He runs a hand down the front of his damp shirt. He pats his stomach, which feels fine. He touches his ear and the flesh around it. That area is still tender and achy, but the pain of it has been so constant he hardly notices it.

"The key," he tells himself, "is not to fall apart right now." He tells himself that he is at a pivotal moment of crux. Should he pass it, he will find himself home free on the other side.

Perhaps he should get the haircut Ms. Malak suggested. He should stop by the dry cleaners, the card of which Ms. Malak left him during her first visit, and retrieve the rest of his clothes. He should make all the little steps he can. The kitten is with a vet. Manal is somewhere in the city. Fadi and his sisters and mother are on the roof. There is some kind of order here. He is part of it, or could be. In any case, he needs to be. He can give them, he thinks, his English and his American name and they can give him a place.

Before he can pull away from the mirror, a memory unfolds without him having bidden it to do so. He knows he could stop it and feels he ought to, but he resists this urge. He sees himself in Los Angeles, walking at dusk. It is between rains, quite cold, and he wears only a T-shirt still wet from the last downpour. Something bad has happened. He has walked so far and so long from the place where the bad thing happened that he feels a little lost; perhaps he means to be. The cold is almost unbearable. The shops are closing, proprietors pulling steel gates across their doors. Nobody looks at him. Outside a hairdresser's shop stands a Latina woman smoking a cigarette.

She turns to go in as he approaches.

Thinking that he would like to sit for a while in the warmth and the light, he asks if she is open.

She tells him she is closing. But then, as he is backing away, she says he looks cold and that she has time after all.

Inside, he sits shivering. Draped beneath the cape, he studies the mirror. The license in its bottom corner is six moths expired. She coughs heavily, then begins to run a comb through his damp hair. The mirror is marked by streaks of gunk, perhaps from her coughing, he thinks.

He answers her question about how he wants it cut by telling her just as it is but shorter.

She is a middle-aged woman, pretty, plump, with dark eyes. He likes the look of her. He likes that she let him in because he appeared cold. He imagines her hands on his head. He imagines he will be comfortable. He hopes the haircut will take a long time, and that she will talk quietly to him and that though he will not really listen to her words, they will soothe him, and he will think of nothing at all but the rhythm of her speech. `

She does not talk. She coughs frequently, and during three such outbursts she drops a comb from her fingers. The first two she replaces from her tray, but then, after she drops the third, she has no more. She picks one off the floor and uses it to finish the cut. He keeps his eyes mostly closed, feeling her cut too close to his scalp. He shuts his eyes more tightly and hums at the very back of his mouth to distract himself from the haircut or anything else which might cross his mind.

Then she tells him she is done.

He knows the cut is bad, so he doesn't look at it.

He takes twenty dollars from his pocket—all the money he has carried but some coins—and hands it to her. "The rest is for you," he says.

She smiles and coughs. She is ten years older than he first thought her. Her eyes are still kind, but he sees in them now something that suggests desperation.

He walks back outside and stops to study the sky and the street. Then the woman comes out with a worn gray jacket she says somebody left once and for which that person never returned.

She tells him again he looks cold.

He takes the jacket and thanks her.

After a few steps, he stops to look in the darkened window of a jewelry store. The gray coat is too small for him so that it looks like a straight jacket he is trying to break out of. Short tufts of hair stand up all over his head. He does not look like himself. He does not look good. He looks so bad he begins to cry. A block later, he feeds some coins into a pay phone.

A voice answers, but in the memory, he cannot hear the voice.

"Listen," he says, "I want to come home."

The memory is finished. At first, he imagines that hearing and recognizing the voice will solve all the mysteries in which he has found himself immersed. Before he can dredge the voice up though, he realizes the memory is an old one and did not immediately or even very closely precede his trip and can tell him little about what he left and why, and, of course, even less about where he is. The owner of the voice comes to him anyway. It belongs to a woman who was not in the list of lovers that played through his mind yesterday. He realizes he can say the name of the owner of the voice and he can also see her face if he wants to. He can tell himself what happened and why he was wandering cold through the streets and what became of his relationship with that woman after the phone call. But it won't matter. It won't solve the mystery of what he meant to leave. He is not here because of that woman, or any other.

This memory is not a key.

A deep sense of disappointment comes over him.

This is followed by a final and frightening realization. It is that no memory will be a key. He could watch the whole of his life on film; he could read a transcript of everything he has ever thought and said, and he still would need some other means by which to get his present bearings.

He realizes he cannot know who he is by recounting what has happened to him.

He realizes, also, that he will not get his hair cut today.

Maybe tomorrow he can be insistent and determined and get to the truth about Ms. Malak and the necessity of the imaginary Dr. Sarkis. Maybe tomorrow he can walk into the neighborhood and find a grocery store he can call his own. Maybe tomorrow he will visit Manal at her work and tell her they should lunch together at a café. Maybe tomorrow he will get his clothes and have his hair cut.

"Maybe, maybe, maybe," he says. "*Yimkin.* Maybe."

Tomorrow

But not today. He has done with it what he can.

As the elevator door opens, he hears his phone ring. Out of breath from running down the hall and bursting through the door, he snatches up the phone and pants a "Hello" into it.

"It is finished," a voice says. It is the voice, he realizes after a moment, of the veterinarian

"What?"

"Finished."

"He's better?"

"He's died."

He waits for the echo of it to raise a feeling in him. No feeling comes. He says, "I'll bring you some money for your work."

"Never mind. It doesn't matter. I'm sorry."

"Yes, me too."

As he hangs up the phone, he feels it. He feels a simple sense of guilt; a simple sense of loss; a simple sense of pain. The kitten has died suffering and alone when all it ever seemed to want was to be next to him. He hurt more than helped it. He should have let it die with him, in the comfort of what it thought it needed, the heat of his body, the cup of his hands.

He looks out at the sea, the water light in the darkness. He thinks of himself swimming on his back out into the salt water, the kitten on his chest, its eyes half closed, the sun bright to keep them warm. He rotates and the kitten goes under. It does not struggle. It dies quickly, without pain or resistance, clinging to him, believing in him. The blue water swells. It fills his eyes and mouth and lungs. It is slightly painful but oddly peaceful. He wishes all the creatures of the world into the calm of the water. Their struggles are muted in the refracted light and swallowed sounds. In three minutes or four it is over for all of them, the birds, the insects, the cows, the cats, the elephants, the people, and everything else. Then there is the question of the water animals. They would live to suffer yet. To snuff them and their potential suffering, he must wish them onto dry land. They flop in the sun, their slickness spreading dark marks across the earth, their eyes black, their mouths, their gills, bursting open, sucking closed, bursting open, sucking closed.

And the vision is no good any longer.

People stand chatting in the parking lot below, which is now two thirds full. Their voices mingle with the voices of people coming from the building across the way—which is half lit in the dusk—and from his own building. Somebody in some apartment below him is playing Arabic music. There is the sound of furniture dragged across the floor above, the pounding of nails in the wall to the side. This place is real; this job is real; his place here is real. And the kitten is dead. And despite the death of the kitten, the people continue to arrive and chat and play their music and rearrange their lives. They have faces he can't see from here, or imagine, but he will go amongst them. He is expected to exist in this context. He expects himself to exist in this context. There is no other.

He doesn't know if he can do it. He doesn't know what not being able to do it will mean. Perhaps this trip itself was the consequence of not having been able to fit himself into some place before. Goose bumps have arisen along the backs of his arms.

He watches a small, very dark woman beat a large rug over the rail of the balcony of the apartment directly across from his. He closes his eyes against the persistent drum of it.

His doorbell rings.

Fadi, Dany, and Nadine stand there, smiling. Nadine hands him an open-topped box of pastries.

"Thank you," he says. "Come in."

"Do you want to come up and see Mama?" Dany asks.

"Up?"

"Yes."

He wants to tell them about the kitten but he knows that even if he gives all the details of finding the kitten and of the night he spent with it, even if he tells the story of the bath and taxi ride and the call he just received, Nadine and Dany and Fadi won't really know about the kitten. Nor will they really know about him.

He can smell the sweetness of the pastries. The light in the hallway flickers, going completely dark for a second so that all three of their faces are in shadows and then the light comes back on. Both girls look beautiful. He has a longing for the beauty, as if he could partake of it in some way he would feel something inside of him had been solved. He can now see faint scars on each of their cheeks. Fadi's are deeper, his face, in fact, is ravished by scars, though his eyes are deep and their lashes long, giving him also a look of beauty. All three have nice teeth. He has the urge to tell them, but he doesn't. He decides against looking at the girls again, but then he finds himself doing it. He cannot help making eye contact Nadine and then Dany. He tells himself that he can appreciate what he sees as beautiful in them without wanting to touch them, that he recognizes and accepts the desire to touch in the face of loneliness as a false solution.

He says, "Yes. I'll come with you. Wait one moment."

He puts the pastries on the kitchen counter. Then he gathers four candy bars left by Ms.Malak and puts a head of lettuce along with two tomatoes onto a plate.

The girls are waiting by the elevator, and Fadi is already inside.

"I'm sorry, I didn't have anything but this."

Fadi smiles and looks away and Nadine follows his gaze. Dany takes the plate. She says, quietly, "Thank you."

They ride down the elevator and walk to the other side of the building and ride up the elevator on that side. He feels at first the pressure to talk—though he can think of nothing to say—but then, long before they arrive, he finds it is unnecessary.

Their mother greets him with a hug, and he finds himself kissing her forehead without thinking about the appropriateness of the action. She accepts the plate and takes it through a little doorway. He tells himself that there is a pureness about this place and these people, and that sitting with them here, he will become pure as well.

They gather on the plastic chairs around the plastic table outside. The Arabic music is clearer now, but the voices of the people are farther away. The sea is visible and three quarter of a moon climbs from the mountain opposite them. It is warm, and something smells good, like lavender. Perhaps it is the girls, though he couldn't smell them in the elevator.

"How is your job?" Dany asks him.

"I don't know. I have an office I can't go into. I have a boss—Dr. Sarkis—who doesn't even exist. It's just a man somebody has made up, I don't know why." He shrugs. "I'm babbling."

"Babbling?" Dany asks.

"It means talking too much about things that are not important. All in all, I think my job is okay. I'm trying to find a way to be okay."

Dany nods.

Nadine says, "But you weren't okay before?"

"No. I don't think so. I don't think I thought so."

Nadine watches his face until he looks at her full on and then she glances away. She appears to study the moon. He can imagine falling in love with her. He can imagine falling in love with Dany instead, or as well. He tells himself love isn't something one imagines. He tells himself that it is possible he will love one of these girls or some other he will meet here or perhaps some other girl he has already met. It will be a good and clean love and he will adhere to it. Nadine glances at him again and this time he looks away.

He wonders things about them all, about their lives here, their lives before now, their lives after now. He wonders how it is they are allowed to stay on the roof, and he wonders if anything will happen to make them go. He wonders if it does, where they will go. He realizes that with time he may know all the answers to these questions. He realizes that with time the lights of the city stretching up onto the mountain will seem like what they are—the light of homes, lights people have turned on against the dark.

"It's lovely," he says. He has the urge to touch any of them, to touch all of them, not in a hungry way, but with simple affection.

"I was taking care of a kitten and it died," he says.

"I'm sorry," Dany says. He can see in her face that she means it.

159

"I didn't make good choices with it. I will have to forgive myself for that."

"There are many things we must forgive ourselves and forget," Nadine says.

Dany nods. She says, "Before the war, we had a house. We had two cars and a man to drive them."

"What happened?"

"They took those things."

"Who did that?"

"The people that took things, the people that killed. Our father was killed. There were people that killed many other and there were people who took things, everything. Nobody knows who they are."

"*La*," Fadi says, "Everybody knows."

"We know who they are *now*," Dany says. "But we don't know who they were then. They don't even know who they were. Nobody knows."

"They are the same now as they were then. And they know," Fadi says. "It is the same inside of them."

"So they are still here, the people that killed each other and stole from each other and hurt the city so badly?" he asks.

"Some of them, of course," Fadi says. After a moment, Fadi asks, "You walked?"

"What?"

"You walked out today and yesterday?"

"Yes."

"You saw them."

"It is true," Dany says. "You see them in shops, on the streets. But they are not the same people as they were. Everybody is new now."

Fadi shakes his head. Dany lets a quick burst of Arabic fly at him. Fadi answers also in Arabic.

Nadine nods toward him and says, "Speak English."

Fadi and Dany go silent.

He says, "I'm sorry for all the things you lost."

"It doesn't matter," Dany says. "There was that life which seems old and there is this life. We're happy in this life."

"Yes?"

160

"Of course," Fadi says. "Very happy." He leans forward as if intent on being taken seriously.

"*Akeed.*"

"What?"

"To say it in Arabic is *akeed.*"

He repeats the word.

"*Akeed* we are happy," Fadi says, leaning back.

"Are you happy, Nadine?"

Smiling, she looks at him. "Yes."

"Mama is happy, too," Fadi says. "We are all happy today. Maybe we will be happy tomorrow."

He wonders if he himself is happy, or if he has been happy, or what happiness feels like to him. Fadi runs his fingers through his short hair. Nadine tips her smiling head to the side. Dany watches him. He thinks of the night before last and how then he felt what he would call happy.

"Fadi gets close to people, to foreigners, to Americans. He does this even though he can tell that they will go," Dany says. "We can all tell the ones who will go."

"What can you tell about me?"

All three look at him. "We want you to stay," Nadine says.

Dany nods, but she closes her mouth as if she is unwilling to say what is on her mind.

Fadi says, "I think you want to stay."

"But will I be able to stay?"

"I hope so," Dany says.

"We will see." Fadi's eyes have dropped. He looks oddly old. His giant face goes slack as if he has fallen asleep or gone into a mime of death.

Dany says, "Never mind. It's all right. You will stay. Tomorrow we will walk with you along the Corniche."

"The Corniche."

"It is what we call the walking place along the sea."

Fadi shrugs and points to the sky, which is clouding. "It will be raining," Fadi says.

The air has cooled considerably. "I guess it is autumn," he says.

"Well, if it is raining," Dany says, "we play Monopoly."

"You have Monopoly?"

"Yes, very old, from before the war. But all the street names are Beirut streets. Many of them are gone now, or not what they were then."

"We will teach you how to be here so that you can stay," Nadine says, dropping her eyes.

He believes her. He is caught up in the idea of their plans. He is caught up with the idea that he can start again, and that he doesn't need to know who he was before.

He says, "You will teach me to be good. Maybe I haven't always been, but that is ok."

They look at him as if he has said something strange. Indeed, he has. He smiles.

The mother brings plates of fruit. Looking at the pieces, he feels a little bubble rise and burst in his gut. Perhaps this is how he became sick to begin with. But he doesn't care. If he is to stay, he will have to teach his guts to accept the food. He eats.

"This is *inab*," Dany tells him

He repeats it.

"And *tiffah*," Nadine tells him

He repeats it and the first again.

"*Ein*," Fadi says, pointing to his eye.

"*Ein*," he says.

"*Keefak*," Dany tells him.

"I know that," he responds. "I should say fine."

"Yes. *Meneeh*."

Fadi goes after pencil and paper and writes these words and others for him.

"He can only learn so much," Dany tells him. "Let him rest."

He is excited. He doesn't want to rest. The music has stopped. People are moving on the Corniche. The sea is dark, the sky as well.

"I'm thinking of a song," he says. "I learned it a long time ago."

"Where did you learn it?"

"When I was young, from my father, he used to like to play it. A long time ago." He can see a child version of himself sitting on a brown carpet in the living room of his childhood home. It is summer and hot; through the windows he can see tall, sharp mountains and a humming-bird feeder. He can hear the song and the voices of his mother and father, sitting on the porch, singing along with the song. He feels threatened by the memory and tries to close his mind to it but can't seem to fully do so.

"What song?" Nadine asks.

"'Eleanor Rigby,' by the Beatles," he says.

He says to them the first stanza. Then he sings the refrain. They watch him as if hypnotized. "Here," he says, writing out the refrain on a piece of paper. "We'll all sing it." He pushes the paper in front of the girls, and they read it over and then as he begins to sing the refrain, the girls sing along with him.

"Come on, Fadi, sing."

They all sing the refrain several times, and then he himself quits singing. He listens. The voices of the girls are quite beautiful. He can't quite make out the words or the tune anymore; he can't tell they are singing "Eleanor Rigby", and yet it is the best he has ever heard it sound. He is aware for a moment that he is not thinking any longer of his parents singing the song while he sat on the brown rug, listening. He is aware that he might never have that memory again. The voices of the girls rise. The mother smiles, nodding her head.

In the silence following he can hear the sea, and the cars driving along it. Clouds overtake the moon. Fadi says certainly it will rain later, perhaps around midnight.

He wonders, briefly, where inside the small edifice they sleep. He wonders where, tomorrow, if it rains, they will play Monopoly. He will have the answers to these simple questions.

"How do you say tomorrow?"

"*Bookra.*"

Tomorrow, he tells himself, he'll learn about the money. He will find out when he is to be paid and how much, and he will find how much cash he has now. He will put things in order.

They sit for awhile longer. Then he feels it is time go. The mother leans against him in a hug. He calls her Mama with a French pronunciation. He realizes he has been doing it throughout the evening, and that he has been doing it not out of an affectation or in some forced attempt to return their generosity, but because it feels natural.

"I'll see you all tomorrow," he says. "*Bookra*. Thank you."

"*Shuqran*," Fadi tells him, "in Arabic it is *Shuqran*."

The downpour begins at midnight. He wakes to acknowledge it for a few moments and then is aware of it in his sleep throughout the night. Inside this awareness grows another one: his guts are twisting in a familiar way.

In the morning, the phone wakes him and he stands at the window through which he can see the sea raging.

It is the deep voice of an older man who identifies himself as Dr. Sarkis.

"You don't sound American."

"I've just woken up."

"You don't sound American," Dr. Sarkis says again.

"But I am."

"I heard you singing last night, and didn't think you sounded American then, either. I was having tea with Captain Shalack on my balcony. We heard your songs."

"Me singing?"

"Last night, from the roof."

"But it was an American song, the Beatles."

"The Beatles are not an American group. They are British. It is then not an American song. Do you want a song from America? Country music comes from America. If you are American, then be American."

"Dr. Sarkis, I wanted to speak to you today."

"And I wanted to speak to you. Do you know, the most important faculty on campus live in the building across

164

from yours? I myself live there during the school months. We could all hear you last night singing. We had higher hopes of you, coming from the States. I myself have been to the States, to Texas, for fifteen years."

"But we were only eating fruit. We were only singing."

"Only this, and only that. How quickly you fell in with them. You know what you would call them in the States? Squatters. With their excuses from the war, with the story about how the husband was killed. He was not killed. He left them for his fear. You can see him in the streets sometimes, begging for money with the others. They've been on that roof quite long enough. I've had a long talk with Captain Shalack about them. And he has had a long talk with me about you. I would imagine you would have known better. A young girl has called on you and been seen leaving your apartment. We hoped you understood you came here to teach these people, not to become one of them. Obviously, you did not understand. Ms. Malak will be by to see you shortly."

"Ms. Malak?"

"Yes. She is coming now to your apartment."

"All right."

There is a pause, and he thinks Dr. Sarkis has hung up, but then the voice comes in again. "We expected more from you."

"Yes," he says, "I'm sorry."

When Ms. Malak arrives, she asks him if his bags are packed.

"No, should they be?"

"Yes." He wants to tell her his stomach hurts. He wants to tell her he is tired and wishes to rest. She stands with her arms folded and her eyes distant, though, and so he tells her nothing.

As he folds the clothes she bought for him into his suitcase, she says, "This is very early for the rain. The lower campus is flooding. Certainly, many of the cats shall be drowned." She shrugs and checks her watch. "It is not proper that they've asked me to take care of you on a day like this.

They give to me too many duties and offer me too little reward."

"Is that what you're here for? To take care of me?"

"Of course. Have you finished?"

He nods.

"Good."

He understands that something of tremendous consequence is happening, and yet he feels nothing substantial in reaction to it. He picks up his suitcase and follows Ms. Malak out of the apartment and into the elevator. He stares at the etches: *Mas Futbal* and *For I Have Seen The Fruits.* A sense of something like nostalgia passes over him and is gone. They ride down in silence. His guts ache. Outside, she unfolds her umbrella and then walks several steps in front of him across the parking lot. He turns several times to look up and see if Fadi or any of his family witnesses his departure, but the roof appears abandoned through the gray slats of water.

She has a small, blue car, and he is embarrassed to get in it because of how wet he is.

"Come on," she says, "hurry up."

He sits with his suitcase in his lap. She pulls out of the guarded parking lot and onto the nearly empty street that follows the Corniche. It is flooded so that sheets of water spray from the front tires. He sits very still so as not to disturb his stomach.

"I know I deserve this."

"Yes."

"I've been bad. I came here from badness."

She does not respond to this.

"Where are we going, Ms. Malak?"

"To the station for the ship."

"What ship?"

"We have booked passage for you to Istanbul. Dr. Sarkis knows somebody with the ship company. He is always owed many favors. He can accomplish nearly anything."

"What am I doing on a ship?"

"You are going. I hope the sea in this weather shall be kind. It seems a not safe time to be making a passage by sea."

"What then?"

"At Istanbul, you have a ticket for a trip by rail all the way to Paris. It is not the famous Orient Express but another company many Arabs use. What a magnificent journey. You are very lucky. Even though you have disappointed us, Dr. Sarkis insists on sending you away in very high style. Plans could not be made to send you quickly to the States. The expense on short notice was immense, and as it happens, Dr. Sarkis knows somebody at the train company. What a wonderful trip. I have all my life dreamed of taking such a trip, but I doubt I ever shall. Istanbul; Bucharest; Budapest; Vienna; Innsbruck; Zurich; Paris. You see, I have the route memorized. Do these names mean anything to you?"

"No."

"They will, I am sure."

He wonders if they will, and if they do, what that meaning will be. They drive along the sea—north or south, east or west, he isn't sure.

§ § §

About the Author

J Eric Miller grew up in the mountains of Colorado and Montana and has since lived, studied, and taught in Los Angeles, California; Grand Rapids, Michigan; Beirut, Lebanon; and Kennesaw, Georgia.

He holds a Ph.D in Creative Writing from the University of Denver and a Master's Degree in Screen Writing from the University of Southern California.

An assistant professor of creative writing in the Master of Professional Writing Program at Kennesaw State University, his short fiction has appeared in a number of print and electronic journals, and his collection of short stories, *Animal Rights and Pornography* was published by Soft Skull Press in September of 2004.